PRAISE FOR BOY KILLS MAN

'This is a fierce, strange and beautiful book, with an unswerving gaze on a terrifying tale. It gives a genuinely human face to a world we would rather dismiss as merely brutal, where the choice is destruction or self-destruction. It captures with great honesty the way weapons can empower those with no hope, and how there can still remain a kind of pride in oneself, even when every door to the future has been closed in your face. Bold, chilling and beautifully written. It really left an ache behind.'
Melvin Burgess

'A powerful, affecting novel about lost youth, and a sharp evocation of one boy's terrible passage from innocence to experience . . . a book we could all do with reading.'
Keith Gray, The Guardian

'*Boy Kills Man* takes a tough, unrelenting look at the nightmare world of Colombian child assassins. Tautly written, giving no hostages to sentimentality at any stage, it is the sort of book that has to be read and then proves impossible to forget. Stunning . . . all that is left is a feeling of sadness and loss. A fine achievement.'
Nick Tucker, The Independent

'Excellent . . . Sonny is a bit like Henry Hill in Martin Scorsese's Goodfellas. It's a shock to realise that his relationshp with Beatriz, the girl he might have loved, has been nothing more than a few shy words'
William Leith, The Daily Telegraph

'Almost causes you to forget that its central characters are only twelve years old. This powerful novel should not be taken lightly.'
Claudia Mody, The Bookseller

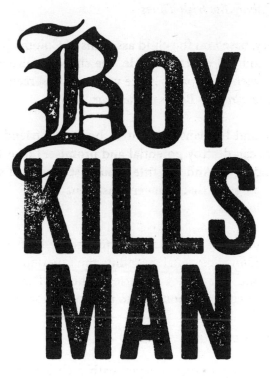

BOY KILLS MAN

MATT WHYMAN

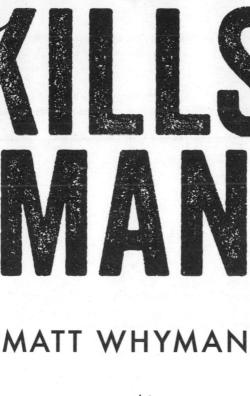

HOT
KEY
BOOKS

First published in Great Britain in 2004
This edition published in 2014 by Hot Key Books
Northburgh House, 10 Northburgh Street, London EC1V 0AT

A CIP catalogue record for this book is available from the British Library.

ISBN: 978-1-4714-0396-5

1

Printed and bound by Clays Ltd, St Ives Plc

FSC

Hot Key Books supports the Forest Stewardship Council (FSC),
the leading international forest certification organisation, and is
committed to printing only on Greenpeace-approved FSC-certified paper.

www.hotkeybooks.com

Hot Key Books is part of the Bonnier Publishing Group
www.bonnierpublishing.com

The Boy

Shorty lives up to his nickname. He hasn't seen the target he's about to take out, but knows it'll be hard to do so with a headshot.

The boy's driver – a man with a sleepy eye, known only as Manu – glances in the rear view mirror. Shorty is slouched in the back there. He has one shoe up on the seat, but Manu isn't hired to teach him manners. That kind of thing was down to his wet-eyed mamà, also the boss man who covers her rent, and little kids like this one always listen to him first. Shorty is wearing cut-down jeans and a white t-shirt, the sleeves folded up like a vest, and he's trying hard to fill it by chewing on a stick of gum. The shirt is way too big for him. So too is the gun in the holster Manu can make out underneath: a 38 Super Auto that the young assassin will have to fire with both hands to counter the kickback.

They're parked in a dusty residential street, with wax palms on each side. The trunks are skinny and skewed, each crowned by green blades that cut up the skyline all over the city. The car is the same kind of green, but for the rust and the mud splats. It's an old Dodge Dart that Manu sometimes drives as an unlicensed cab. Even with the windows down it reeks of sweat, tobacco and air freshener. If they have to wait any longer, thinks Manu, the stink will kill them before the heat.

1

It's two o'clock in the afternoon, and a brutal sun keeps most people indoors. The only activity takes place up ahead, where a knot of older kids flick a soccer ball among themselves. Shorty has been focused on them since they pulled up. In his dreams he'll play professionally one day, for Atlético Nacional, Medellín's number one team, but right now the drug inside him stops his feet from becoming too itchy. Shorty has a job to do here, after all, which is why Manu had injected him minutes earlier with two mills of the anti-panic medication he keeps in the glove compartment.

Man, too much of that gear could send them straight to sleep. It was just a question of keeping them focused without watering down the natural adrenalin that turned the little ones into live wires. In the right hands, it could be a lethal combination. That the law wouldn't jail a minor for a murder made them ideal for the job. Unless the government lived up to its half-assed legislation, and took hired guns like this one under its wing, well, the street would always take care of them. They got protection this way, and even a purpose in life, which was more than the state could offer. Sure, some rehab centres had been opened up to save such delinquents from themselves, but nowhere near enough to cope with demand. Abandoned but untouchable, these kids made perfect killers.

Voices emerge from a lobby just then: a couple in conversation. Shorty switches his attention to the concrete block across the street, hears Manu confirm it's him – the fool with the loose mouth. They see a middle-aged businessman come out of the building, and agree it must be his wife behind. He stops to say a few parting words to her, slings his jacket over one shoulder and heads right, just as Shorty has been briefed. Manu turns to face the boy, and finds him chewing on his gum more furiously than ever. All kids were like this for a while. Trouble only happened when they grew tired of what they were doing, or figured they could call the shots, but this one has some way to go yet. Twisting round now, Manu reaches out of his window and springs the passenger door. The child lock is a pain, but it guards against a change of heart.

'It's always good to be a little scared,' is the last thing the boy hears him say. 'Just make it clean for the boss, if you can. You might even earn yourself that season ticket he's been promising.'

1

'Believe me, nothing is more unsettling in this world than a kid with a gun.' That's what the boss says whenever he introduces me to people. I've never found myself on the wrong side of a piece, not for real. Then again, I suppose you could say I'm the kind of kid people fear.

'An adult is aware of the consequences,' he'll continue, so softly you almost have to hold your breath in case you miss something. 'He's likely to hesitate before pulling the trigger, or scale down the hit and just scare the sucker instead. A boy doesn't think like that. You give him a job, he'll get it done, no question. Why?' He always pauses here (or pats me on the head if I'm standing right beside him), 'Because a boy is aware of the consequences if he *doesn't* see it through.'

My boss has the quietest voice you ever heard. Some say that it sounds like a deathly whisper, which is why he is known as *El Fantasma* – The Ghost. It also means that when he speaks, everybody listens. I need a gun in my hand before I can earn the same attention, or some money wrapped up in a band. The first time I told my mother that she no longer needed to go out each night to work, she just blinked at me. It didn't matter how many times I said I could take care of things, my presence in the apartment was all she seemed to take in.

Things changed once she had time to think. Now, if I place some cash on the table, Mamá clutches her forehead with one hand and blames herself for all kinds of things. If Uncle Jairo is in earshot then he'll get involved, too. My uncle has bad lungs, which is why he's always so frustrated and short-tempered. He reminds her I'm thirteen this year, almost a man. If I'm so smart and wise with words like he's always hearing, then why hadn't she sacrificed everything to keep me off the streets, huh? So shut up for once, he'll spit, and let your son repay us for bringing him up. Sometimes Mamá will start wailing, which makes him scream bad things at her before panicking because he's mislaid his inhaler. By then, I can't even remember the point she'd been trying to make. *El Fantasma* wouldn't allow things to get out of hand like that. He always has complete control of any situation, whether he's scolding his guards or telling a funny story. He would make a great coach, I think. Give him eleven men, and within a season he'd shape them up into God's own team.

The boss has always known me as Shorty. It's something I got called one time and annoyingly it stuck like gum to a shoe. It just doesn't suit any position on the pitch, you know? If Shorty were in goal, you'd simply aim high to get the ball in the back of the net. Place the little guy in defence, or midfield, it would be a question of using your legs to outrun him. I suppose it doesn't sound so bad for an attacking player, but not as proud and formidable as Sonny, my real name. A memorable striker needs no surname, and Sonny just says it all.

. . . *the ball swings up to Sonny, and the crowd are on their feet! The whole of Medellín are behind him. He's passed one, two, and he shoots . . .*

It was Papa who named me, two months before I was born. I'm told he was utterly convinced that he would have a son. My mother claims he even described how I would look as I grew up. According to her, he hasn't been wrong so far. If this is true, he must also have been aware that he would never see his predictions made flesh. All I know for sure is that Papa had to leave home in a hurry, though nobody ever explained why. It could've been the cops were after him, or maybe the cartel. I've learned not to ask any more. It just makes people angry – or sad. Either way, it must have taken a lot of courage, saying goodbye to his wife and unborn child. Only a brave man could make that kind of sacrifice. I just hope he foresaw that I would inherit his great courage.

. . . *Gooooaaaalllllll!!!!!!*

El Fantasma shares my passion for soccer as well as for Nacional. I heard he is on personal terms with the trainer there, and has a seat in a bullet-proof box. The boss can handle a ball too, even if he is a little chubby in the face and waist. He likes to play with one touch, just like our national side. Some say it's an arrogant style, but if the team play as one it can be deadly.

'Always keep the ball moving,' he tells me. 'You can't afford to give the opposition time to react. If the dust has settled and you still have possession, you're in trouble.'

Alberto played a very different style. If my best friend won the ball, which he often did without waiting for a pass, you could be sure he wouldn't give it up. Instead, he would thunder for the box and nobody dared get in his way. Players sometimes stepped aside for him, just as they did for *El Fantasma,* but this was because Alberto was built like a *bull*. I used to think he charged in all the time because he was too ashamed to call out for the ball. You would expect a kid our age to squeak a bit, but Alberto had it bad. For a boy who looked like he should growl and grumble, it could come as quite a shock.

'So what if my *huevas* haven't dropped yet?' he once piped up. 'What matters is they're made of steel!'

We had a lot in common, Alberto and I. We grew up in the same *barrio,* and lived to support the same team. We could never afford to see Nacional play, but that didn't stop us spending every home game in the shadow of the *Atanasio Girardot*. I have never been inside this stadium, just as I have yet to travel beyond the city limits, but I often dreamed about what it must be like. We would bring a football with us, of course, and knock it around on the concrete as if the crowd in there were roaring for us.

We always made sure we were on the same side, too. If I was picking a team, Alberto would be my first selection and me his. No question. Unlike most kids, however, we didn't belong to a gang. In Alberto's opinion, that kind of thing was for cowards who couldn't fight for themselves.

'Never rely on other people if you want to get on in this life,' he told me once, which was easy for him to say. Despite the difference in our size, we thought of each other as blood-brothers. We just didn't have the scars on our palms to prove it. Often stuff went unsaid between us, but even though I only came up to his chest we *always* saw eye to eye. My best friend was a big baby, a big boy, and would've been a mountain of a man. He had a face that went wide when he grinned, and always had his hair pulled back in a fierce pigtail We took communion on the same day, and grew up listening to the same bootleg tapes. First Elvis rocked our world, but then Nirvana came into our lives. We listened to everything by them that we could lay our hands on, but privately I liked the quieter songs the best. I didn't like to admit this to Alberto. I worried that he might laugh and accuse me of being a sissy, even though the stuff they did with acoustic guitars had more power and force than anything else. If my father ever returned, I used to think to myself at night, he would look like Kurt Cobain.

Music, money, Jesus Christ and soccer: that's what made our world go round, and for me it hasn't stopped spinning.

2

On the streets and on the pitch, Alberto and I were a team. My friend was younger than me by two months, but he always led the way for me to follow. One week after he gave up on school, I decided to join him running cigarettes across the city. I was used to being picked on by my classmates because of my size, but without Alberto the taunts had quickly turned to serious threats, and so I decided to go. We got the work from a man called Galán who owned a general store opposite our block. Galán liked to make out he was an old style *contrabandista* who had laundered vast riches in his time. That he struggled to keep his shelves stocked made us think he was basically well connected with his imagination, but we let him have his moment as it paid us cash to burn.

"This isn't just work I'm providing,' he crowed when he first took us on. 'It's an education!'

I didn't like Galán much. He wore an aftershave that smelled like sugared almonds, always had one finger curled around a fat cigar and kept mentioning that he once served up party food for Pablo Escobar. What the boastful old goat seemed to forget was that anyone in this city who made a living in the Eighties and early Nineties probably did so thanks to the same man.

Most kids in this country know about history. We aren't told fairy tales at bedtime, simply because the real-life stories of courage, treachery, bloodshed, love and honour have so much more to offer. It helps that we have TV, too, even if a lot of stuff about our past is made in the USA.

Take the documentary I once saw about Escobar. It claimed that the billions of dollars he made trafficking cocaine cost our country its soul. Now, everyone accepts he was prepared to go to great lengths to protect his business interests, but all animals have a heart. That's how Alberto once put it, and he was right. Pablo loved Colombia with the same passion that he loved his family, and Medellín was his home. Without him, thousands of people would have no roof over their heads, no hospice beds or nurseries, so I can understand why many still weep at his grave.

Alberto and I couldn't hope to remember the day he finally got cut down, but the stories about him crossed into folklore. Maybe some of the truth got a little twisted along the way, but then he was a complicated man from a complicated place. You only have to consider our politics to see that we're screwed. The old folk who spend their days playing chess in the park? They know about these things. Give them a chance and they'll quickly leave your head in a spin. They'll go way back fifty years and more, to a time when the two main parties conducted themselves with dignity, like rival teams on the pitch.

The conservatives and the liberals relied on reason and debate in their battle for control of the country, with no foul play. Then came the assassin's bullet, one with a popular leader's name on it. That marked the end of one era and the beginning of the next: *La Violencia* – in which our country turned against itself, and tore everything apart. Some say we have yet to recover from those ten savage years of uprising, strikes and guerrilla warfare. Sure, there were stabs at restoring calm, but then drugs became big business and that storm has yet to end. Those old guys who have lived through it all can tell you how cocaine caused the two sides to splinter into countless groups, but even *they* can't say what cause anyone is fighting for any more. Seems we've been at war with ourselves for so long that nobody knows the difference now between power and peace.

The only certainty is that the gun speaks louder than words.

Every day I hear the crack of a pistol, or get word of a kidnapping and ransom demand. Gangsters rule here, not government, though it's sometimes said that a lot of police and politicians are criminals who haven't come out yet. Medellín may be kind of wild around the fringes, but then it isn't a lawless place to live. If someone has done you wrong, there are ways and means of getting justice. Even if you can't afford it straight away, terms can be arranged.

There are plenty of good times to be had here as well, particularly on the pitch, and lately I've noticed that we have the most beautiful girls in the world.

Mountains also surround our city, and that can't fail to lift the spirits. From the roof of my apartment block, looking out over washing-lines and TV aerials, you get a clear view of forested slopes and gullies, even snow-caps sometimes. We spent a lot of time on that roof, Alberto and me. Nobody could touch us there, and we could only be seen from the sky. It's also where we hid the packs of cigarettes skimmed from Galán, and learned to smoke like soldiers.

'Some day we'll get to the top,' Alberto once said to me, and flicked his dog end as if it might make it to the looming summit. 'We'll steal ourselves some motorbikes and take ourselves all the way up there. I've always wondered what it looks like on the other side.'

The money we made from Galán wouldn't get us far. That miser always haggled with us whenever we returned with the goods, which was why we skimmed the smokes. Even so, we always accepted more runs from him. We were ten years old when we started out, and though he paid us peanuts it seemed a lot to boys like us. We weren't exactly made of money, after all. We came from El Diamante in the southern quarter: a poor part of an impoverished city, but not the worst. Without work, we would've been forced out beyond the slums and the shanties, to the garbage heaps in the hills. My mother would've raged and wept at this, just as she did soon after *El Fantasma* found me, but I had to pay my way. That was the understanding, maybe not with her but certainly with Uncle Jairo. I've seen those skinny thieves up there, competing with the vultures for food and trinkets, and I realise how lucky I am. I earn some money, but a great deal more in respect. *Nobody* calls me Shorty outside of the compound, and our neighbours quit telling dirty lies about my mother some time ago. They know what I can do, and wisely they leave us in peace.

Without Alberto, most probably I would be picking through the trash already. I may not play by the same tactics as my friend: on or off the soccer pitch, I don't run with the ball until someone takes me down, but I *have* learned to make my mark. Sure, he had some weight to throw around, but it doesn't matter how you shape up on the outside. It's courage that counts, and Alberto brought that out in me when we decided Galán should pay for ripping us off.

'The sonofabitch treats us like kids,' he moaned, and spat on the ground between his feet.

'That's because we *are* kids, Alberto. Face it.'

'But we're doing a man's job. Guys three times our age run cigarettes and get a bigger cut for it. Why should we settle for coins? It isn't right! We should show him, Sonny. We should make him pay. If we don't get the respect, soon everyone will treat us like bitches.'

Alberto and I had always steered clear of trouble. We left that kind of thing to the rival gangs, let them square up to each other while we got on with living. Now my friend had landed me with little choice. I didn't want him to think I was a coward, just as I hated the idea that Galán might be laughing behind our backs. The plan we cooked up seemed like a quick and simple way to save face. I wasn't going in alone, after all. Alberto would be with me every step of the way.

You should've seen the pair of us, crossing to his store with our shoulders squared and faces set. I closed in on the door first, mainly to hide the fact that Alberto was clutching a baseball bat. He told me he had borrowed it from a neighbour in our block. I figured that meant he had stolen it, and was lucky not to have been caught. In this city, a bat was for protection only.

'Are you sure about this, Alberto?'

'Keep moving, man,' I heard him hiss, sounding supercharged. 'Don't stop now.'

We were here to do business, not run stupid errands, and if Galán didn't see reason then we would make a mess of his store. Privately I didn't think it would come to that. I figured he might even admire us for standing up for ourselves, and agree to the wage we deserved.

What we hadn't considered was that Galán would have company: some skinny guy with his hood up and his back to us, facing him across the counter. It was cooler inside, out of the sun, but it didn't stop my skin from prickling. The *contrabandista* looked up at me without moving a muscle, which seemed odd and even alarming. Then I saw that the skinny guy was holding a switchblade to the soft part of Galán's throat, and I froze just like him.

3

One glimpse of the blade and I pulled up, almost backtracked. We'd walked into a robbery, but as the skinny guy was across at the counter we had a chance to walk right out again. I was about to spin on my heels, but the door I had just pushed open hit the stopper with a bang. The guy twisted around at the waist: pasty-faced inside that hood, with eyes that darted between us.

'Scram!' For a moment, he snatched the knife away and showed it to us. I thought the storekeeper might come over the counter at him, but his gaze just followed the blade back to his throat. 'Go home, little boys.'

We were nothing to him. Two kids come in for provisions, sent here by our mothers most probably. That's how it must've seemed, which gave Alberto a big advantage when he shoved me aside, already bringing the bat around with both hands . . . *whump!* The guy took the hit in the stomach, and almost folded over. His head appeared to pop out of his hood, a look of shock and horror in his face, while the breath left his lungs in an awful bark. Alberto snapped the bat away and he just crumpled. It was his jaw that took the full force of a second blow – this time from an upswing. His head snapped back too far, spittle flying high, but Alberto hadn't finished. As the guy went down, he began to kick and stomp on him as if this was a fire that had to be put out.

'Enough, stop now!'

The voice seemed to come out of nowhere. I barely recognised it as my own, but somehow it got through to my friend. Alberto stood back, panting, and the bat just dropped from his hand. Galán remained frozen behind the counter, staring wide-eyed at Alberto – this express train that had come through his door.

'Mother of Christ,' he breathed, 'what have you done?'

The guy on the tiles was making an unholy mewling noise now. Even when he seemed to run out of air it just went on and on. His head was half turned inside the hood, and the side of his face that I could see was bloody and out of shape. He was sprawled on his back with one arm flung backwards, the blade resting uselessly in the palm of his hand. For a moment I thought he was trying to say something. I saw his lips part, and that's when I found his line of sight. I could've been looking at one of the fish we used to land, all the life left in it sealed inside one eye. He was easily into his twenties but seemed younger than me just then: nothing more than a terrified little street punk who didn't want any of this. Then the noise he was making trailed away and I watched his gaze fall slack.

I couldn't blink. I couldn't speak or breathe. I just stood there with my hand across my mouth, wishing we had never come into the goddamn store. Minutes earlier, we had stood in the alley round the back, pumping ourselves up, but not for this. Outside, people went about their business. The sun was shining, and swifts could be heard twittering from the telegraph wires. The *barrio* was always a busy place, and nothing had changed that now. The only difference was how still and silent it was here in the store.

'Is he dead?' This was Alberto. He sounded all slowed down, like a tape-player running on old batteries.

'He will be.' Galán reached for the telephone on the shelf behind him and dialed out a number from memory. With the receiver lodged between his shoulder and his ear, he turned to the drawer under his cash register and drew out a large cigar. Just like that. Not even a glance back at the body on his floor.

'What now?' I asked, trying hard not to let my legs give way. I felt sick, as if I had just breathed in something evil.

'What do you think, "what now"?' Galán paused to fire up his cigar. 'What now is this prick goes to Hell.' He broke off there, greeted whoever it was who'd picked up the call. The way he turned away with the receiver, I realised it was meant to be private. I looked at Alberto. He was still just standing there, struck dumb it seemed to me. I reached out and touched his arm.

'It'll be all right, man.' I said weakly, and cleared my throat before trying again. 'Everything will be good again.'

'Hey, fellas!' Galán broke off from his call, sounding cross with us all of a sudden. 'Will you move him into the back room? C'mon, what are you waiting for?'

Obediently, Alberto dipped down and grabbed the guy by his ankles. I had no idea what was going through his mind. I was just glad to see him moving. I took his wrists and together we hauled the body across the tiles. Galán continued to chatter on the phone. As we reached the door behind the counter he cut us a frown. It was as if we were dealing with a sack of rotten watermelons here, messing up the tiles. I looked straight ahead all the way through, hoping and praying that this terrible weight between us wouldn't suddenly twitch or make any more noise.

Later, when the flatbed truck pulled up outside the store, followed by a silver 4x4, I would hope and pray that he really *was* as dead as can be. Galán had hurried us from the building just as soon as the body and the bat were out of sight. As we left he kept saying that we should go home and tell no one.

'This didn't happen,' was his final word to us, and at the time I almost believed him.

Leaving the store was like waking from a bad dream. The air seemed so fresh that Alberto and I just stood in the street for a beat and breathed. We both turned with a start when Galán shot the bolt across the door. He flattened his lips at us, there behind the glass, and then flipped the sign from OPEN to CLOSED.

We didn't go home, of course. We took the fire-stairs round the back of our building, and headed straight for the roof. There, we sat against the old extractor hood and smoked some cigarettes. Every now and then, one of us broke the silence with a cough or a muttered *'mierda,'* but we never looked at each other for more than a moment. I didn't want to see what was going on behind Alberto's eyes, and I was scared for him to see into mine. We only stirred when the truck turned up with the big jeep behind it, and that's when it seemed very real. Peeking over the parapet, we saw two brawny guys climb out of the flatbed and haul a tarpaulin roll off the back. They could've been anyone, a couple of rough hands like almost every other migrant in this *barrio,* but the man from the 4x4 didn't fit. He was wearing a light suit, white sneakers and shades, and moved like someone who didn't like to dwell too long in one place. I was sure he was going to peel off those glasses and look directly up at us. Instead, the two goons carried the tarpaulin into the alley beside the store and the man followed behind. A side door opened up and we watched him hustle them in, looking left and then right before disappearing from sight.

'Galán wasn't lying,' Alberto whispered, as if he might be heard even from here. 'He really is connected after all.'

4

There are two types of people in this city: the poor who scratch a living on street level, and those who have turned to the underworld to survive. Not everyone does so willingly, of course. For every drug don there are dozens of everyday citizens who have decided that it's better to accept a bribe than see their loved ones go missing. The cops and the judges may be decent people at heart, but with that kind of choice it's no wonder so many take the money. Most of the time you can't tell who has links and who needs some.

We always thought Galán was a bullshitter until he made that call, but it seemed Alberto was right. You only had to look at the party who came to collect the body to know where they had come from. These guys were *gangsters*. Not just street hoods grouped together for safety, but the kind who pulled all the strings in this city. Watching them leave the store from the front, with that tarpaulin roll looking a little heavier now, I felt both terror and awe. They left as quickly as they had arrived, with no fuss or fanfare. Galán waited for the silver jeep to pull away after the flatbed, and then flipped the store sign to show that he was back in business.

The events of that afternoon went down deep for us both. It became a part of who we were. We never once relived what had happened in that store, and I didn't ask my friend how it felt to kill a man. I figured it was probably the same for him as it was for me: something that we couldn't talk about because neither of us knew where to start. At first we spent a lot of the time not saying very much at all, just hanging out together, but as each day passed we found our tongues again. When our money ran short we even went back to the store. What's more, Galán began to pay us the extra we had wanted for every carton of cigarettes delivered. He even trusted us with unmarked packages and packets, and stopped shooing us away whenever the phone rang. A few weeks later, it became clear that he had spoken highly of us both. For that's how *El Fantasma* came into our lives.

I had never heard of the man when Alberto mentioned his name. Even so, it was clear by his gift to my friend that he had influence and power.

'What do you think of me now, eh?' Alberto was standing square to me on the roof, as if preparing for a showdown. 'Isn't she something?'

'It's a gun,' I stated, half laughing.'It isn't real though, is it?'

Alberto stood down, invited me over for a closer look. It was black, silver and stubby. A semi-automatic, I knew that much. I had seen gang members make it obvious when they were carrying, and on instinct I always stayed clear. I was never scared, just cautious, but now here I was up on the roof with my very best friend. I just couldn't keep my distance from him, even with this weapon between us.

'Take a look at her,' he said, again like it was a girl, and showed me the magazine. I got a glimpse of the bullets racked up inside before he slammed it back into the grip. He seemed very confident, as if someone had shown him how to handle himself. 'She's a Smith and Wesson,' he told me. 'A real beauty.' I watched him weigh the pistol in his palm, wondering where this woman talk had come from. Then his fingers curled around the grip and trigger, and I found myself directly in his line of sight. 'On your knees, now.'

I looked up smartly, grinning because Alberto's voice had cracked when he said this, and a cry died in my throat. He was pointing the gun right at me, not finding this funny at all. His eyes narrowed into slits, only to finish it as suddenly as it had started by cocking his elbow so the gun was out of my face. I breathed out and thought I would never stop.

'Jesus, Sonny.' Alberto melted into a loopy grin. 'You just messed your pants!'

'No, I did not!' My knees felt like curls of butter, but I also felt stung and that kept me on my feet. Alberto was my friend and friends did *not* pull stunts like this. 'What's going on, brother? Where did you get the money for a goddamn gun?'

'Didn't cost me a single peso.' He reached for his back pocket now, pulled out five ten-dollar bills. 'This guy paid me to look after it for him.'

'In dollars? No way!' I was beginning to get that sick feeling in the pit of my guts once more. American currency wasn't supposed to be good here. You couldn't spend it in the shopping malls, but then it bought you a lot on the streets. Everyone knew how it had come into the country, of course, which is why it was also worth a great deal in respect. 'Come on,' I pressed him again. 'What fool was dumb enough to tool you up?'

Alberto gestured over the edge of the building, to the store on the opposite side of the street. We were supposed to work as a team for Galán. I had never been in there alone, and when I thought about what he meant I felt a bit betrayed.

'Our infamous *contrabandista* called me over this morning,' he explained. 'Said an associate would be visiting him in the hour who wanted to talk to me'

'And give you a loaded piece,' I cut in. 'A kid like you, just like that? C'mon!'

'I swear it on my life, Sonny! I feel like a *bandido,* man. The real deal.'

I frowned, wishing he would wise up, but still couldn't help thinking he should've waited for me. I had been helping Uncle Jairo all morning, acting like his second walking stick while we shopped for groceries. Alberto didn't have the same kind of ties. His mother pretty much lived in the textile factory where she worked several shifts from dawn to dusk, while his sister spent her days at college. He never really talked about any other family, but then I was only interested in the one I sometimes saw clutching text books to her breast.

Beatriz was sixteen, four years older than Alberto and the family's shining star. She had the brains where he had the brawn, and everyone said that one day she would be a doctor. Their father passed away many years earlier. His death had been slow and certain, a cancer of the blood that reached his liver. He had insisted that Beatriz did not abandon her studies for him, and so it fell upon her little brother to nurse him during the day so his mother could continue to provide. It meant the two of them were confined to a house that felt more like a waiting-room. With time on their hands, Alberto's father chose to fill it by schooling him in something, even if it was just stories.

In particular, Alberto loved to hear about the *bandidos*, and I wasn't surprised that the gun had reminded him of them. These were outlaws who had become folk heroes – men such as Sangranegra, Desquite and Guadalupe Salcedo – all of whom had earned their reputation during *La Violencia*. Each commanded a band of thieves –ruthless renegades who ran rings around what was left of the establishment and stole a place in the hearts of the poor. As his father's end drew near, however, Alberto confided in me that he was beginning to suspect some of the tales he heard seemed so rich in feeling and finish that they had to be confessions. I told him, don't be dumb. His papa would've been a kid our age when these guys roamed the hills, but Alberto seemed to cling to the belief that he was the son of someone very special.

My mother once told me this had been Alberto's way of coping with the loss when it finally came, so I never raised the subject again. I figured he'd grown out of it, but now I saw how alive he looked with a gun in his hand. It was as if he had found his calling somehow, a chance to follow in his father's footsteps – even though his old man had conjured up that path from his deathbed.

'Alberto,' I said finally, and waited until I had his full attention. 'Do you know what you're getting into here? This isn't like the old days. We don't have heroes any more, apart from on the pitch.'

'Listen to you, *Senor* Sensible.'

'I just can't believe some guy paid you to take his gun.'

'Why not? He didn't ask me to use it. I'm just minding it for him, I guess.'

'Why couldn't he stash it, same as any gangster?'

'Who says he's a gangster, and anyway what would *you* have done, huh? C'mon, Sonny, I didn't have much choice. I showed up at Galán's like I'd been told, got shown into the back room and there he was. Sitting at the table with a coffee and the early edition of *El Colombiano*. I was only in there for a minute or so. He asked if I wanted to make some easy money, and just came right out with the gun before I could answer. He told me all I had to do was prove I could be trusted to look after it. I couldn't exactly walk away, but then I didn't have a problem with staying. I just see the fifty bucks he lays down next to the piece, already I'm thinking about how I can spend it.'

'*El Fantasma,*' I said to myself, chewing on the nickname. 'What is he, some kind of spook?'

'That's not our business,' Alberto said with a shrug, 'but let me tell you, I never heard a man speak in such a whisper.'

5

The woman peered at us from behind the toughened glass. Alberto had just dropped the money into the hatch for her to draw through, but something stopped her from collecting it.

'What's the matter?' he asked talking like a tough guy. 'They're dollar bills. Dead presidents, every one of them.'

She held his gaze for a moment longer, then sighed and took the money. She gave us some funny looks still, along with a lot of pesos in spare change and two very precious tickets.

'I cannot wait until next month!' Alberto practically danced away from the box office. He even kissed the foil-stitched slips before handing one to me. We were going to see Nacional for the very first time. It would be the opening fixture of the season. What's more, we were playing Medellín rivals, Independiente, which meant it would be more like a fiesta than a football match. If all the Feast Days could be rolled into one, and the saints were given a soccer ball to celebrate, this match would be it. The city would go *wild,* and I could not wait.

'I'm not letting mine out of my sight,' I said, as we rattled down the steps outside the stadium.

'Don't keep it in your hot little hand,' Alberto joked. 'The ink might run.' He was wearing a money belt under his vest, and patted it now to show me where he had just put his own ticket for safekeeping. He had found the belt some weeks before, lying in the street. It was empty, of course, and the clasp had taken some fixing from where it had been ripped from the previous owner. I had told him anyone dumb enough to wear such a thing deserved to be robbed, and back then he'd agreed. Now he had been paid to carry a gun. Like the tickets he had just bought with the money, Alberto couldn't afford to let it out of his sight. Watching him fuss with the belt one more time, I figured it had gone to his head.

'Alberto, that sticks out a mile. You could be robbed.'

'Not if I get to it first,' he said, and used his fingers to fire off some imaginary shots. 'Come on, let's get a taxi home.' I was about to remind him that the money wouldn't last for ever, but Alberto was already on the sidewalk with his hand raised high. 'I want to visit the florist and then on to see Mamá. I never bought flowers for her before. You should do the same thing, Sonny. I'll lend you the cash if you like.'

I stayed outside when Alberto walked in with the lilies. The factory where his mother machined pillowcases for a living wasn't much bigger than Galán's store. It was south from our block, further downhill, with a grille across the window that was too high for me to peek inside. Alberto had said his mother would most probably cry and he didn't want anyone else to see that. I waited there with my back to the wall, cupping my eyes from the sun. After a minute, however, I had to turn – not because of the glare but all the shouting that had just started up. Alberto left like a grenade with a stuck pin. He slammed the door shut behind him, his face and ears flushed red.

'I should've just showed her how I got the money,' he spat, his voice pitched high as ever. 'That would've shut her up.'

Part of me wanted to go back and tell his mother that I would talk some sense into him, but I didn't dare upset Alberto any more. I followed him up the hill, struggling to stay with him. It was close to midday, and the heat had already pushed most people inside. The volume always dropped at this time of day, apart from the dogs and parakeets, which is why we both picked up on the fact that a motor was slowing behind us. I glanced over my shoulder. It was a green Dodge that had seen better days, though the throb and growl from under the bonnet made it clear this was a muscle car. You could always hear them coming in this city – standard issue vehicles with a beast of an engine packed inside. A plastic Madonna hung from the rear-view mirror, along with one of those freshener things that sometimes made me feel sick. The driver had the window down already, and as the Dodge drew level it seemed that he was looking right through both of us. It was only when he called out to Alberto that I realised one eye looked a little dead.

'Jump in, *hombre*.'

Our street smarts told us to ignore him, even though he was cruising right beside us now. We weren't dumb. A stranger offers you a lift for no reason, he wants to interfere with you, hold you to ransom or murder you – sometimes one after the other.

'*Alberto*,' the man barked, 'do you hear?' My friend swung around at this, still moving with me but looking less sure of himself. 'I don't know you, man.'

'Boss wants to see you. He says to bring the heat you've been minding.'

Alberto stopped, as did the Dodge with a rasp of the handbrake. I hung back as my friend went across to him, feeling awkward and uneasy. The driver was way into his fifties, and looked as worn out as his car. He was wearing a short-sleeved shirt with pelicans and palm trees on it, but his mood was far from sunny. He spoke a few words to Alberto, jabbed a thumb over his shoulder and my friend just left me there on the sidewalk.

'I'll see you later,' he said, ducking into the back seat. All the fury in him from that row with his mother had gone now, and I wondered if I should go fetch her. I waited for him to roll down the window, thinking he might tell me to fetch help, but all he did was look out at me.

The Dodge moved off with a lurch, quickly gathering speed. I watched the car make the corner, Alberto looking straight ahead, and then the street was empty again: silent but for a barking dog and a crappy radio coming out of an open window.

People always say that springtime lasts for ever in Medellín, so when the hot days hit, the city simply stews. My clothes clung to my skin that afternoon. Even the walls inside our apartment looked like they were close to breaking into a sweat. The place was exactly the same as all the others in the *barrio*: one big room divided by curtains and screens. I had gone back there to fix up something to eat, and just knew that Uncle Jairo was in before opening the door. I had heard him hawking and spitting up phlegm from the street, which didn't do much for my appetite. My mother was shopping for groceries, so he said, which meant he was free to hassle me about where I'd been and what I was doing with my life.

I sliced up a mango and took it to the window ledge with some salt and a fork, but wasn't in much of a mood to talk. I kept telling myself not to worry about Alberto. He knew what he was doing, just as I was sure I could've taken care of myself in the same situation. I was a bit put out that I hadn't been invited along for the ride, which is why I wanted to finish eating without being hassled by my uncle.

'Your poor mother.' That was what he always came back to, like *he* wasn't mostly to blame for the fact that she had to work twice as hard to keep him. 'Did she bring you into this world just so you could depend on her for food and a place to sleep? I think not, Sonny. Jesus Christ, look at you!'

My uncle was all smoke and no fire. He just kind of smouldered day and night. He certainly sounded like he was all burned out on the inside, the way he cursed and coughed and wheezed. We shared some family features – same build and untamed pride – and you only had to look at our saucer ears to see that we were related. But that's where the similarity stopped. His skin was paper-thin and ashtray grey, while every bone in his body seemed to be a source of misery when he moved. OK, he had breathing difficulties, but it was his bitterness about it that caused the most suffering. Sometimes I wondered if the man had a good word to say about anything. If he wasn't bitching at me he was moaning about *los americanos* – who he blamed for his lot in life.

It didn't stop him from watching their soap operas and sports, but he always did so like it was a punishment, not a pleasure.

'Know your enemy,' he once advised me. 'Even if you have to learn to live with it.'

Uncle Jairo had come here to stay when I was five, at a time when he could barely speak because of what had happened to his lungs. He had been working in the south of the country on a coca plantation. To him, like most labourers, the crop was just that: a bunch of leaves bound up with twine that paid for their food and lodging. What happened to it afterwards was not his business, but the Americans didn't see things that way. They had pledged to destroy such a crop at source since it began to arrive as a powder on their street corners.

The attack happened close to harvest. My uncle had been appointed to check for weed and signs of infestation: anything that might harm the coca leaf. The plantation clung to a steep slope, almost a ravine according to Jairo who always liked to talk it up. He claimed that working there could cripple even the fittest, most upright men, but that's not what he blamed for his condition. According to his account, he had noted the distant drone but didn't react until a machine gun woke up the valley.

He knew there were nests around here, set up by his employers, but had never expected to see so much gunfire spit from the trees. As the shots rattled out all the birds in the valley took flight, but it was too late for Jairo to follow. By now the incoming noise was almost upon him, and peaked when a small aircraft sprung over the ridge. It banked low across the plantation, before pulling up and turning corkscrews into the sky. Shocked and in a spin himself, my uncle had taken a moment before registering the drizzle that fell in its wake. It had an oily feel between his thumb and forefinger, he said, and a strong chemical smell. That's when he came to his senses, covered his mouth with his shirt and ran. Every worker in the plantation did likewise, but it was too late to escape. All of them came down from the fields with streaming eyes and a cough some said could never be cured.

That day, word was that the Americans had destroyed a dozen plantations in the region: spraying each one with a pesticide many call poison. The coca lords simply moved deeper into the mountains to start again, but Jairo didn't join them. With his health doomed, he had no choice but to turn to his closest family member for support. He made his way to Medellín, a journey from hell so he claimed, only to find his brother was no longer with us.

Uncle Jairo looked very different back then. When he crouched to shake my little hand, I even thought my father had returned. It was his explosive coughing fits that made me wary, but they were enough to persuade his sister-in-law to take him in.

Before his arrival, our neighbours had considered my mother to be widowed. Maybe they just pitied her predicament, but still they treated her with due respect. All that changed, however, once my uncle began to eat his meals at the head of our table, and went on to share her bed.

I would lay down my life for my mother, as any son should, but I would do nothing for the man who stole her heart from his very own brother. Such is the shame he brought to our house that my grandparents and several cousins disowned us completely. I just wish I could've done the same thing. Instead, he became all we had. At first it was his wheezing lungs that scared me, but even after I conquered that he remained a monster in my eyes. The weaker Jairo became, the more he saw me as a threat to his place in the home. Mostly I could switch off from all the hassle he directed at me. But the afternoon Alberto took off in that Dodge, as I worried about my friend and even what I had missed out on, my uncle got right under my skin.

'The way you run away from your responsibilities, Sonny, it's an insult to the family name.' That was what he said, almost spitting the words over my plate. I looked up, found him picking his ear. 'You're so like your father, I guess that's no surprise.'

I didn't know what he meant, but I still kicked back my chair and reminded him that he had no right to speak like that here.

'This was my house first!' I snapped, squaring up to him now. 'It doesn't matter how long you've been here, you'll always be the uninvited guest!'

For, a second Jairo looked stunned, even when he climbed to his feet. I just stood there and let him rise over me, amazed that I had silenced anyone, if only for a moment. Then I took a punch to the side of the head and ran for the door before he could see how much it had hurt.

Alberto was the only person who never judged me. When some of the kids in the *barrio* once dared to suggest my mother scratched a living by selling her body to businessmen, he straightened them out right away. It didn't matter that he sounded like Mickey Mouse with a bad attitude. It was his presence that persuaded people to leave it alone.

'You got something to say to my friend,' was all he had to say. 'First you clear it with me.'

Alberto had issues of his own at home, but nobody poked fun at his family. I felt safe being with him, and wished he was around as I headed out into the heat. I was mad with my uncle, but I couldn't go back inside now. Not until my mother was home to keep the peace between us.

It wasn't the first time Jairo had hit me. My uncle liked to use his fists when words failed him, which they often did when his lungs let him down. I took a whack from him most days, but this was the first time I had earned it by standing my ground. It left me feeling shaken but surprised at myself. Just like when Alberto and I had left Galán with a body in the back room.

I drifted for a long while, wishing my ear would stop stinging. Eventually I wound up watching the game going on in the cage behind the pool hall, and that took my mind off things. The cage was supposed to be for basketball, but the hoops had been stolen long ago. It wasn't that great for soccer, either, what with clumps of weeds in the cracks, but the high fencing made up for that. A lot of guys from the market liked to come out here when they could, which meant a never-ending game took place with players coming and going all the time.

Nobody asked me to join in, of course. I could've shown them a trick or two had they given me a chance, but to them I was just a kid: some nobody on the wrong side of the fence, chewing at his thumbnails and kicking up grit. Alberto would know to look for me here, but after an hour I grew tired of waiting. I figured Galán would know where he was, but as I reached his store I found I couldn't bring myself to enter. One glimpse through that door was enough to spook me, and I walked on by with my head down.

I was cross at myself when this happened, and all the more determined to make my mark on the day. That's why I decided to make sure I had some money in my pocket before I looked for my friend again. It wasn't hard to earn a few pesos, no matter how bad things got around here, especially if you had a skill. Like most boys my age, I knew how to strip a motorbike for spare parts. It was just a question of asking around at the market, and making a nuisance of myself until I got the work I wanted. My hands were filthy by the time I tracked down Alberto, but I had some coins in my pocket to show for it.

As it turned out, my friend needed to clean up more urgently than I did, while the cash he had to show me simply took my breath away.

6

'It's done now.' This was all he would say when I asked where he had been, and even then he refused to look me in the eye. Alberto had answered my knock at the door, and then walked right back into the kitchen area with my question chasing after him. I found him standing at the sink, with his back to me.

'Man,' he muttered next, 'I need a smoke.'

'I can buy some,' I said brightly, and dropped my stash of pesos on to the table. Alberto had the sink tap running and was scrubbing at something with a nailbrush. He was still wearing that money belt of his, his vest all caught up in it at the back. When my coins hit the surface he glanced over his shoulder, but didn't seem as pleased as I had hoped. I asked him what he wanted: Hidalgos or Lucky Strike? Alberto said either would be good, and some cigarette papers for the grass he had in his back pocket.

'You got dope?'

'Is what I just said, dumbass.'

'Alberto . . .' I trailed off there, tipped my head to one side. 'Is everything OK?'

One time we had made a delivery to the airport for Galán, and earned ourselves a ready rolled reefer as a tip. Our contact there said he could always help us out on that front, and even some powder if we were interested, but we never went back for more. Alberto had been eager to fire up the joint on the way home, but after a couple of hits he let me smoke the rest. It clearly hadn't gone down well with him, and I quickly realised why. Now here he was inviting me to get some papers so we could both feel quietly sick all over again.

Alberto reached for a dishcloth, and I pressed him to explain what was going on.

'It's a gift. No big deal. What else could I do? Say no?'

'Like you couldn't say no to the pistol?'

Now he turned to me, and I realised he'd been trying to scrub his vest. Alberto looked like he'd eaten a jam waffle in too much of a hurry, but the fierce scowl on his face told me not to question it. All the time he just carried on drying his hands – endlessly turning that cloth until I thought he might start shredding it. Maybe he sensed my alarm, because he lightened up with his next breath, and offered to get the cigarettes himself.

'Keep your cash,' he said, and pulled a fold of dollar bills from that damn money belt. 'I just need something to sort me out, all right? Beatriz will be back soon, and I don't want anyone to see me like this but you.'

There had to be one hundred, maybe one hundred and fifty bucks there, and for me that was more than enough. My friend had spots of blood on his vest and a look that told me something very bad indeed had occurred that afternoon. I really didn't know what to think or say. I just took the money he offered me, told him I would see him on the rooftop once I'd picked up the cigarettes and the papers, then left.

I would go straight to bed that night without anyone knowing that I had come home. My mother had yet to return herself, and I found Uncle Jairo dozing in front of a bullfight on the portable. It was the only source of light in the room as the bulb had blown again, which meant shadows blinked and shuddered all around me. I was used to it, and for a while I just lay on my bed and listened to the commentary. I hadn't smoked as much grass as Alberto, but I certainly felt the effects. It wasn't so bad this time. In fact it had been a nice way to see through the dog end of the day. At first Alberto had been so on edge I didn't think he would stay for long. He kept fidgeting and cracking his knuckles, then complained that it was too quiet. The first joint seemed to sort him out, however, and by the time I stubbed out the second one we were happy just to sit back and watch the sun sink behind the mountains.

After that we just wandered through the *barrio*. We hung out by the pool hall, watched a dice game going on outside, and finished up eating cold chicken wings that Alberto bought for us both. I waited for him to tell me what had happened that afternoon, but either it was no big deal or he still had to make sense of it himself. I figured he would tell me all about it in his own time. I had never kept a secret from him, after all.

'What shall we do tomorrow?' I asked, as I licked the grease from my fingers.

'Let's just see what it brings,' he had said, like he couldn't be sure the sun would ever rise again. I caught his eye, thinking maybe he would tell me now. Instead, he tossed the box away, burped and patted his barrel-like belly. He was still wearing his money belt underneath, I noticed, though I didn't need to be reminded of the gun he had in there with his ticket and all that money: 'All I know is it'll be one day less before the match, Sonny. One step closer to the greatest day of our lives.'

My uncle had an attack in the early hours of the morning. I slept right through, the dope must've sent me down deep, but fortunately for him my mother was back. According to her, Jairo awoke shortly after she had turned in. He opened his eyes, saw the TV had been shut down, then tried to call out when it seemed his lungs had done likewise. Mamá had stirred when he crashed from his chair. She found him clutching at his throat as if supernatural hands were trying to strangle him. His inhaler saw off that demon, though when I heard what happened I did wonder if perhaps my father had come home in spirit.

Old Jairo was still out for the count as I ate my breakfast, and so my mother and I spoke quickly and in whispers. I guess we each had our reasons for not wanting to wake him.

'Are you going to school today, Sonny?'

She asked me the same question every morning, as if school was just an option. I hadn't been inside a classroom for two years, and the more time passed the harder it became to give her the real answer. Alberto figured she preferred to fool herself because it made everything feel safer. That's why I said, 'Sure I am' as I did every day. Only this time, I followed it with a question of my own. 'Do you still think about Papa?'

She was warming a pan of milk for the coffee. At first it seemed she hadn't heard me. I realised I had kind of sprung it on her, but it was on my mind and I needed to know. My mother had rich chocolate hair that she only ever wore down after dark. Just then, as she poured the milk into two cups, I noticed grey licks coming through under the clips. It looked nice on her. Made her seem as old as the world, like she'd be here for ever.

'I pray for him,' she said eventually, and nodded to herself as if at first she'd hadn't been sure of her answer. 'Just as I pray for you.'

Alberto lived two floors below me. I could make it down there in six giant leaps, so long as I didn't swing off the rail at the foot of each flight. If he didn't answer when I banged on the door then I would often just let myself in. I had a copy of his key, just as he had one for our apartment. Usually it meant he was in but still in bed, but I was always happy to wait until he surfaced. His place looked just like mine, except it didn't have my uncle in it. As a result, I was free to listen to the radio or spend time thinking without being threatened with a kick up the ass.

Of course, I would never walk in without making a big noise. I didn't want him to stir thinking that a thief had crept into the place, nor let him off lightly for being so lazy.

'Eh, *vagabundo*, it's me! Stop drooling into your pillow and get your big fat pants on.' I strode in chuckling to myself, only to catch my breath at the vision that shrieked and darted behind a partition.

'*Sonny!*'

I spun around to face the door, horrified at myself.

'I saw nothing,' I lied, cringing now. 'Well—'

'My God, get out of here!'

I had just set eyes on Alberto's older sister, her hair all wet, clutching a towel to her naked body. She hadn't even wrapped it around her waist, just held it bunched against her belly. I felt like I had just startled an animal so rare that it was hard to be sure I had seen it at all.

'Oh, Beatriz, I'm so sorry. Really. I was looking for Alberto.'

'Obviously,' she replied from behind the partition. 'You half frightened me to death, barging in like that. What were you thinking?'

'I apologise,' I said struggling to focus on the door. 'I didn't expect you to be in.'

'I'm on exam leave, like that's any of your business.'

'Ah. Can I look now?'

'No!'

'Is your brother here please, Beatriz?'

'He left early, even before Mamá. I assumed you'd be with him, like always.'

'Not today,' I said eventually, trying hard to sound breezy. Beatriz was only a few years older than Alberto and me, but she was shaping up into a fine-looking young woman. I wasn't sure what rattled me more: what I had seen or what Alberto was up to without me once again.

'OK,' she said, sounding warmer now. 'You can relax.'

Sheepishly, I turned back around, and wished my face didn't feel so warm. Beatriz was standing there in a Nacional shirt that almost fringed her knees, drying her hair now with the same towel.

'I always thought that shirt belonged to Alberto,' I said, struggling to find something to say.

'It does,' she replied. 'But then I did just have to dress in a hurry.'

'I'm sorry.'

'Stop saying that!'

I grinned at this, and so did she. I thought about saying it suited her better, but my nerves got the better of me. On Alberto, the vertical green and white stripes could make him look like an over-stuffed tube of toothpaste, but on Beatriz it really did look just right. She had coal dark eyes and long hair to match, with a fringe cut high that was new, I thought. Normally I managed to be relaxed around Beatriz, but then I had never paid her this much attention before.

'Sonny,' she said again, as if to stir me from a spell. 'You can go now.'

'Oh. Sure.' I found the door handle and stepped back on to the landing. 'Sorry,' I said again, for no particular reason, but it sounded like I was apologising for my very existence.

'I'll let him know you called,' she said, holding back a smile now. 'Have a good day, Sonny.'

'You, too. Happy revising.'

'Er, thanks,' she said, and closed the door.

For a beat I just stood there, and winced as I heard the bolt shoot. 'Happy revising?' I muttered to myself this time. 'Oh boy, you have a lot to learn.'

Had Alberto been around just then, he would've made my life a misery. I could've expected an entire morning of grief about how I had handled the situation. I even knew what he would say.

So you busted in on my sister in the buff? You be sure to completely erase that moment from your memory, do you hear? Beatriz is way too good for you. She's older than you, and way out of your league like most girls round here.

Chances are I would've protested my innocence, and then finally laughed about it with him. Instead, I had nobody but myself for company, which didn't amount to much.

Alberto clearly had other things to do: a purpose to his day. He had people to meet, contacts who relied on him to get a job done, and paid out serious money. What did I have? A few pesos in my pocket and a lot of hassle back home.

By the time he caught up with me, watching the soccer behind the pool hall, I was feeling very left out and bitter about it.

'Hey, kid!' he flopped down beside me now, face up into the sunshine. Alberto had never called me this before, unlike most people in the *barrio*. I didn't make a big deal out of it. I just hoped it wasn't going to become a habit. 'My sister left a note,' he said next. 'Apparently you called round earlier.'

'That's right.' I said nothing more, just hoped that was all she told him. We sat there in silence for a moment, following the match. There wasn't much skill going on here, just a lot of men past their prime flocking after a football. What they needed was new blood: a couple of players to shake up the mix a bit.

'Shame you weren't with me this morning,' he said next. 'We could've had a blast.'

The offer seemed a bit late to me. He knew where I lived, after all.

'Dirty work?' I asked, with both eyes on the ball.

'Huh?' I sensed him turn to face me, but carried on looking straight ahead. I was busting to ask how many bucks that gun of his had earned once again, but first I needed to remind him we were supposed to be a team. 'Sonny,' he said next, 'what is your problem?'

'Depends on where you've been, I guess.'

'You wanna know?' he said, raising his voice now. 'I've been uptown, OK? I went *shopping*. I spent the rest of my money on a new vest to replace the one that got all messed up yesterday, plus a nice new shirt and stuff. I just felt like some treats, that's all. I didn't think I needed your permission. What's got into you?'

I looked across at him now, tried to match his glare. Alberto never lost it with me, not before now, and for once I saw what a threatening presence he could be. Sensing that threat grow, I said: 'Let's leave it. Just forget we even had this conversation.'

'It's forgotten,' he said, but stayed right where he was. I could see that he was thinking things through, reading my face for some kind of answer. 'This is about the gun again, right? Jesus, Sonny!'

'Yesterday, you came home with blood on your shirt and a pocketful of money. I'm no fool, Alberto. I see there's a link between the two. I just want to know why you won't tell me.'

'Because there's nothing I can say!' he snapped, but stopped himself from going on. He took a breath, and began again. 'I can't tell you anything,' he said, calmer now, 'because if I open my mouth I'll be dead already.' His eyes remained fixed on mine, urging me to understand. They swore me to secrecy, Sonny, and I've got to respect that. Please don't ask me, man. Just understand.'

'Who are "they"?'

'The people I'm working for,' he said abruptly, his eyes pinching at the corners. 'The same people who paid me to do a job so I could buy two tickets to the match. One for me, one for my best friend. Now shut up with the interrogation, and quit mothering me.'

'Sounds to me like someone has to.'

'I am *not* a child any more. How many more times, Sonny? I can handle myself.'

It was then he showed me the holster. It was strapped high under his shirt, the gun slotted neatly inside, and I knew for sure that he had left me behind. I only caught a glimpse because he was quick to cover it up again. I looked up, as surprised as I was when he first showed me the pistol itself, and saw that he was grinning.

'The holster was one of the other things I bought,' he said. 'I can reach it quicker like this.' He patted his side, the bulge showing through. Next he searched his pockets and pulled out two lime-green lollipops. 'These were the other thing,' he said, turning all goofy as he offered one to me. There used to be a time when we would spend what pesos we had on sweets. If we had no money we would often try to steal them. We found that made them taste even nicer. 'I bought a whole box of them,' Alberto told me, and ripped off his wrapper. 'I think we deserve it.'

I wished I could've felt the same kind of buzz, but I wasn't the one who was packing. I just bit down on my lolly so I didn't have to hold the stick, and was pleased when he suggested that we track down a game we could both join in.

Alberto said he'd caught sight of a good one on his way here: a gang we knew from our *barrio* who often found themselves short on numbers.

Maybe it was the opposition, or just the fact that he had a gun under his shirt, but Alberto played a mean game that day. Every time I passed him the ball, he took it as far as he could. One boy who dared to bring him down found himself marked so hard he never got another touch. Not until Alberto left the pitch, at any rate. I didn't see him go. I was too busy in the box, but when I looked around I realised we were one man down. When I asked if anyone knew where he went the keeper joked that his boyfriend had showed up in a beat-up muscle car and the big guy had gone running. I didn't laugh like everyone else, but nor did I defend my friend's name.

7

Alberto left me to my own devices another two times that week. The week after, he went off on three occasions, maybe four, and then I stopped counting. The big match was looming, after all, so I began to strike off the days instead.

Mostly the man with the dead eye and the green Dodge would call him away, but sometimes he'd be gone before the break of day. I'd call round first thing to find nobody home but his sister. Even though I learned to knock, she always found me flustered. She was nice, Beatriz. Most girls her age peered down their noses at a boy like me, but not her. Still, she'd give me a look whenever I asked after her brother. It was a look that told me she knew something was going on with him, but couldn't make any sense of it. I wanted to tell her it was the same for me, but only once got further than drawing breath.

'What can I do?' I blurted at the time. 'I'm his best friend, not his father!'

'I know that,' she had said, sounding calm and kind. 'But you're the next best thing to him. Alberto would come to you if he was in trouble, so if there's something you want to share, Sonny, I'm here.'

'Sure,' I said, partly because I'd had no choice but also because it made me feel so special.

I never mentioned this promise to Alberto. I didn't even like to tell him that Beatriz and I often chatted when

I called round. I was worried that he might start asking why I was so interested and then give me hell because she was his sister and I was a kid and *blah blah blah*.

Besides, whenever Alberto did show up he was rarely in a mood to shoot the breeze. Each time, he seemed to come back a different person: like a clockwork toy that had been wound up a turn too tight. I'd ask him about his day and he'd just bounce me into another conversation about a bootleg tape he'd seen on a stall, or a likely soccer transfer before the season started. It sometimes took him several reefers to calm down, but even then he wasn't himself. He would become almost too quiet – so lost in thought that I wondered if he would ever find his way out again. It never lasted long, he usually slept it off, and the next day his confidence would return in force. The way Alberto had been built meant he was naturally larger than life, but now that came with a swagger. He walked tall, chin up, in a way that I couldn't quite match. I tried to copy him but it didn't feel right. I figured it would take some practice, but only when he wasn't around.

All this time the money kept coming in, and Alberto proved to be a generous friend. One evening, I was killing time up on the roof when he appeared carrying a ghetto blaster. Brand new. Box fresh.

'Tell me you haven't just carried that through the *barrio!*' I declared, amazed when he said that he had. 'Man, the thieves in this city must be losing their touch.'

'People leave me alone,' he told me. I knew what he meant, and felt foolish for trying to make fun of him. Only recently, some of the kids around here had noticed

Alberto climb into the Dodge three days running. They began joking that Alberto was sucking dick for a living, but that came to a complete halt when word reached Alberto himself. Maybe they found out how he was earning his money, but it certainly earned him a vibe that demanded some respect. I just felt privileged when that vibe began to rub off on me. Galán even came to find me about running more cigarettes and actually offered to pay even more because I would be working alone. Galán must've known that Alberto had better things to do, but I took on a couple of runs to show I could be trusted just like him. Wherever we went inside the *barrio*, people treated us differently. It wasn't much, just a look or greeting, but it felt as if we were somebody, and I soon stopped feeling so sidelined. If anything, Alberto made every effort to share his good fortune with me – like the stereo that he had just set down at my feet.

'It's a gift,' he said, leaning back against the extractor hood. 'It's about time we had some music up here. Maybe some of that stripped-down shit you've been liking on the sly.'

'Alberto, I can't accept this. It's too much.'

I was gawping at the offering when a CD clattered into my lap. *Nirvana: Unplugged in New York City.* A live acoustic session. Not a tape, or a pirate copy, but the real deal.

'Take it,' he said, when I protested again. 'Else I'll be offended.'

That evening, I felt like I was looking out across the rooftops from a throne. We fired up the stereo, worked out how to put the beat box on repeat, and then listened to Nirvana and smoked and tuned out of the world around. Everyone knew that the singer Kurt Cobain had taken his own life. According to the guy who sold the CD to Alberto, he had turned that shotgun on himself soon after the gig recorded here. That just made me listen to it more closely, wondering if he knew at the time that his end was near. He certainly didn't sound sad or frightened, just calm and a little jaded, like someone looking forward to a long sleep.

Firecrackers filled the silence between each song. They had been going off every sundown for a while now, and sounded exactly like gunfire. Maybe bullets featured in the mix, but there was no mistaking the *fiesta* spirit that was beginning to seize the city. The bunting was out all over the *barrio*, and people had made arrangements so they would be close to a television or a radio set come Saturday. We had no need to make such plans. For when Nacional played their first match of the season at the weekend, we would be there to cheer them on.

'It should be like this all the time,' I said to Alberto, as another song closed. We were lying flat on our backs now, watching points of light break out above.

'Damn right,' agreed Alberto. 'I imagine it will be if we get a win.'

I hadn't even considered what the result would be - hadn't thought further than the kick off – but now I started thinking way beyond the match. Eventually, I said:

'What do you want to be when you grow up?'

'I am grown up,' he said, still focused on the stars.

'You know what I mean. And don't say a striker because you know that's my ambition.'

I heard him chuckle, and then fall quiet. Kurt was singing over another volley of crackers about a man who sold the world. The guitar sounded shaky and unsteady in places, but that made it seem more real to me.

'You know what I want to be most of all?' Alberto said eventually. 'I just want to be safe.'

'From what?'

I turned so I was resting on my forearm. Alberto took a breath, and glanced across to check that he had my attention: 'I keep dreaming that I'm running away from something. I can't tell you what it is, because whenever I look over my shoulder I see darkness.'

'It's just a nightmare,' I said. 'We all have those.'

'Sonny, this one comes to me so often it doesn't even scare me any more. I dream I'm fleeing for my life, and that my only escape is to wake up. Just once, though, it would be nice to dream that I was running *towards* something. I don't want to be so uptight about what's behind me all the time, do you understand?'

I wasn't entirely sure that I did, but I nodded anyway. 'It'll happen,' I assured him. 'It'll happen for us both, brother. We're going places already.'

Alberto sighed, and heaved himself into a sitting position. He lowered the volume on the stereo, looked out towards the scrapers. They stood like tombstones at the centre of the city, hemmed in by the sprawl.

'If Mamá finds out I got a gun,' he said next, 'the only place I'll be heading is Hell.'

'You sound scared?' Now it was my turn to sit up.

'I'm not scared of what she'll do to me,' he said quickly. 'I'm just worried what the truth would do to *her*.'

'She'd freak out, for sure.'

'Freak out? It would *destroy* her, man, and that would be my fault. Her only son, packing a piece.'

'I won't tell a soul,' I said to reassure him. 'I swear it.'

Alberto shrugged, and lit himself a cigarette. 'She won't take any money from me,' he revealed. 'I've stopped offering it to her because all she does is look at me like she's going to cry, and now she's started searching through my stuff. Yesterday, I came home to find she'd taken my room apart and put everything back just how I had left it.'

'Alberto,' I laughed, 'she probably just dusted! It's no wonder you're having bad dreams. You need to calm down.'

'I've got a *gun*, man! That's not so easy.'

'Then let me look after it for you.' I didn't even think before I said this, but it was too late to take back. Just for one night,' I added. 'So you get a good night's sleep.'

Alberto stared at me, considering what I had said, and then looked away shaking his head. 'It'll give you bad dreams, Sonny. I guarantee it.'

'I can handle it, Alberto. Trust me!' Now it was my turn to speak out. For this would be the perfect way for me to show that I was just as capable as him. Alberto may have been the chosen one, but it would prove that we were still equals. 'Come on, brother. What do you say?'

'I say you're crazy, Sonny. But you know what? I've been losing so much shut eye lately that it sounds like a good idea to me.' He unbuckled the holster as he said this, and I felt my heart begin to race. 'You've got to promise me you won't fool around with it – don't even take off the safety catch. They've been counting the bullets see, just to make sure I haven't been working for anyone else.'

I went from hot to cold as he handed me the holster, again when I touched the pistol grip. It felt surprisingly light, like a toy, though Alberto seemed to think otherwise. He rolled his shoulders, said it was a relief to get the straps off his back.

'Shall I wear it?' I asked. The truth was I didn't know what to do. I felt like I had just been handed a newborn baby. I had no idea how to hold it, and pretty much froze up.

'*Shall I wear it?*' he repeated, mimicking me. 'No, Sonny. You take pot shots into the street until someone shoots back at you. Of *course* you wear it! Under your shirt, nice and tight so nobody can see.'

Alberto buckled me into the holster, and made me swear on my mother's life that I would just forget about it. Then he finished by promising to be at my apartment first thing to collect it from me. 'So there goes your chance to come round and score on my sister,' he said, with a wink.

I stood up, feeling dizzy. The dope wasn't helping, and that last jibe of his had come out of nowhere. Even so, I was determined to show that I was in control here. I was the one with the weapon now, not him. I had a *gun*, with bullets in the clip. I had never felt such a sense of exhilaration. I had never been so scared of myself either.

'Don't forget the beat box,' he said. 'It's yours, remember.'

'Alberto, why don't you take it home?'

'A gift is a gift,' he insisted, dropping down to collect it for me. 'But if it makes you feel better, think of it as payment for one night's peace of mind.'

I hit the stop button, found the handle, and together we left the rooftop in silence. The city remained restless, as it always did on a balmy night, only now I felt as if I was at the very heart of it.

8

'Sonny? Was it you making that almighty racket on the roof? Show yourself, boy!'

This was my welcome home, before I had even closed the door behind me. I knew my mother was out because Uncle Jairo was watching TV with the light off again. It sounded like a talk show – one of those trashy ones where everyone shouts and my uncle felt he had to do the same rather than turn down the volume. I pushed through the curtain, found him nursing a beer at the table. He had the window wide open, but I was surprised he could hear anything outside. The glare from the screen made his long face look all milky, and threw his shadow across the wall behind him. On the show he was watching, two women were screaming at each other. They looked close to a catfight, and the host was having some trouble keeping them apart.

'Uncle Jairo, I'm gonna turn in. Could you quieten it down a little?'

'These bitches need a real man to sort them out.' Jairo said this without taking his eyes off the screen. At the same time the host made some lame attempt to intervene, only for one of the guests to shove him hard in the chest.

'Are you gonna let her disrespect you like that?' Jairo almost knocked his beer off the table, then seemed to recognise he had just lost his cool with a television tube. He dragged a palm from his brow to the back of his neck, and shifted his attention towards me. I was still holding on to the curtain, half turned so he couldn't see me properly. Alberto had assured me that the holster was invisible under my shirt, but it still felt like a hot brick to me. As a result, I completely forgot what else I had come in with.

'Show me that.'

'What?'

'The stereo dumbass.' Jairo gestured at the beat box, then waved me closer. He seemed a little unsteady, not drunk but on the way. 'Let me see what we have here.'

'It's mine,' I said, thinking if I handed it over I'd never see it again.

'Sure it's yours.' He paused to take a slug from the bottle. 'So my brother's boy has turned to *thievery* now? I knew this day would come.'

'I didn't steal it,' I said hotly. 'It's a gift from Alberto. He sort of . . . bought it for me.' The more I tried to explain myself, the worse it sounded. I began to wish I had told him to mind his own business, but it was too late for that now.

'So what? Is Alberto your boyfriend all of a sudden?' Jairo seemed amused for a second, but then he started coughing and that wiped the smile from his face. Finally, he grabbed enough breath to demand the stereo. 'C'mon, Sonny, are you deaf as well as queer?'

'Turn down the TV and I might be able to hear you insult me a bit better!' For a beat, it seemed like even the women on the screen fell silent. Jairo just looked up at me, no longer coughing but wheezing heavily, and then made a vague attempt to stand.

'Do you need your cane?' I asked, hoping to gloss over what had just been said.

My uncle nodded, eyes down now, supporting himself with one hand on the table. 'That would be good,' he said, and stayed stooped there as I fetched it for him.

I didn't think either of us wanted to fall out all the time. It seemed so pointless, a war that neither of us could win because we'd only destroy my mother. I collected the cane from the corner of the room, and guided both his hands to the crook.

'Just take it easy and get your breath back.'

He thanked me twice, reached up to his full height, and for a moment I thought he was falling into me.

The blow got me in the chest – a two-fisted sock with the crook in-between that knocked me off my feet. I fell back into the curtain, bringing it down with me. The stereo hit the floor at the same time, and that was when my uncle started yelling over the TV.

'*How dare you play the big man with me, Sonny! When will you learn that I'm the man here, understand? I . . . am . . . the man!*'

I knew he was going to hit me again. I thrust out my hand, but he kicked it away. Uncle Jairo had a clear advantage, and not just because he was standing over me. He got me in the balls next, so hard I curled up like a salted slug. The pain swam into my stomach, up my back, and left me writhing pathetically. Even though my uncle was sick, I was no match when his fury took a hold.

'*I pity your father, giving birth to a loser like you . . .*'

He cursed and swore at me with every strike, and went on to scream about my mother, too. He was careful to avoid my face, I realised, but I only had two hands and that wasn't enough to shield the rest of my body.

Then he began to use his shoe heel to stamp on me, and I thought about the gun.

I could feel it underneath me, digging into my back. A voice in my head screamed at me to reach round for it and take out that sucker. There was no way I would let him finish me off like this, after all. I wasn't going to leave the world in the same way as that thief had left Galliano's store. I was a fighter. And like Alberto, I just wanted to be safe.

'*You stupid, goddam son of a whore . . .*'

I knew I was capable of squeezing the trigger, but I had made a promise to my friend. That's why I kept reminding myself that this was just a punishment. Jairo wasn't dumb enough to kill me here, or leave a mark I couldn't hide, so I bunched up as best I could until he had finished.

'Damn it, now the stereo is bust,' he wheezed eventually, and gave me one last, half-hearted kick. 'Why is everything made so bad these days?'

I heard him drop back into the chair, and wrestle with his inhaler. The women on the TV were still arguing, the audience behind them now. I didn't move from the floor. The pain from where he'd caught me in the *huevas* had turned my stomach to stone, and my sides felt like they'd come apart if I stopped hugging myself. All I could do was fight for breath, just like my uncle, and feel the curtain underneath my cheek grow damp with tears.

'I'm sorry that it's come to this,' I heard him say next, only to break off and cough into his fist again. 'Just show some respect in future. You're twelve years old, damn it. A kid your age shouldn't have to be told twice. Just because you're smart, doesn't mean you can be a smartass, understand? Your mother thinks you got an old man's head on your shoulders, but I don't hear old men going on and on and on. They know when to shut the hell up, Sonny. How else do you think they get to their age?'

When I felt sure that he was through with me, I crawled off the curtain and took myself to bed. I couldn't say whether I passed out straight away or a long time later. Either way, all I could hear was those two women warring – the volume racked up by another notch.

I stirred next morning to hear Uncle Jairo and Alberto at the door. I didn't open my eyes, just listened. My uncle was speaking in a forced whisper, and seemed annoyed that Alberto wouldn't follow his example.

'Sonny had a bad night and needs to sleep,' Jairo was saying. 'I'm sure he'll call on you when he wakes.'

'Please,' Alberto piped up again. 'It's important that I see him now.'

'Will you 'keep the noise down!' hissed my uncle. 'If you disturb his mother too, then God help you. Now stop being a prick and go home.'

I wanted to get out of bed, but my body didn't feel right. Sure enough, when I tried to sit up a charge flashed across my chest that reminded me what had happened. Next I heard Alberto click his tongue and tell my uncle he'd be waiting for me. By the time I made it out of bed, Jairo was back behind the kitchen table. He was wearing his spectacles, and had the stereo in front of him. One side of the plastic housing was all smashed, and he was covering it with strips of parcel tape.

'Your boyfriend called,' he said, without even looking across.

'He isn't my boyfriend. Please, Uncle Jairo.'

'Whatever. '

I stood there clutching my sides, feeling too weak for another fight, and turned to look in on my mother. Their room was on the other side of the curtain divide, and I was surprised to see the bed empty.

'I heard you say she was sleeping.'

'Maybe I did.' Jairo chuckled to himself. 'Whatever Alberto thinks of me, I'm damn sure he respects your Mamá.'

'So where is she?'

'Out.' He looked up at me, startled at what he saw, and quickly returned to his work. Why don't you go back to bed, Sonny? Rest yourself a while.'

'What time did she come home last night?'

'She'll be home later, Sonny.'

'Uncle Jairo—'

'That's *enough!*' he slapped his hand on the table. It made the stereo jump as well as me. 'Why do you have to cross me all the time, huh? She's probably at church, OK? Praying for your sorry soul.'

'Probably? I don't believe you.'

'Fine. You want the truth? She didn't come home at all last night. Seems she likes her job too much. Now get out of my sight, because I swear I'm in no mood to be reasonable today, and when your mother does get in she'll be sorry, just like her son.'

I was thankful that Alberto answered the door when I called for him, and not Beatriz. I was in the same clothes as the day before, the gun still strapped in the holster. In truth I wasn't sure I could get it off. I had been too dazed to try the night before. Now the searing pain in my ribs stopped me from finding the buckle.

'Sonny!' he said brightly, and stepped aside for me. 'Your uncle said you'd had a bad night. Are you ill? You look like you've been puking, the face on you.'

'It's nothing like that.'

I heard him close the door behind me, and winced when he clapped me on the back. 'So, what happened?'

'I had some problems getting to sleep, I suppose.'

'Told you.' Alberto invited me to sit down at the table, grinning as he took the chair opposite. 'Man, that gun is guaranteed to keep you staring at the ceiling all night, but I appreciate you taking it. I slept like a big old baby. It was sweet, some of the things I dreamed about.' And that's where he stopped, because I wasn't laughing with him. 'Do you want some coffee?' he asked. 'Everyone is out this morning. I figured we should bring the stereo down, or maybe watch some cartoons for a while.'

'Sure,' I said, thinking I might cry. I tried hard not to meet Alberto's eye, but he was waiting for me to look at him. When I glanced up finally, he swore under his breath.

'The gun. You've still got it.'

'Of course.' I patted my side to reassure him. 'Alberto, stop staring at me like that. Everything is fine.'

Alberto blinked and stepped back at last. 'Well, I appreciate you looking after it. If you ever want me to do something for you, just say the word.' At the same time, he gestured for me to hand it over. I bit into my lip and reached around for the clasp to the holster.

'Here, let me help you with that.'

Before I could stop him, Alberto had come round beside me. I tried to stop him from lifting my top to find the buckle, and that's when he just took over.

'Mother of God, what has happened to you?'

'Nothing.' I tried to pull away, but he wouldn't let go.

'Sonny, those bruises . . . was it Jairo?'

'No!'

'Yes, it was. Of course it was him! Don't lie to me, Sonny!'

'I can handle it,' I pleaded, again when he snatched the pistol from the holster. '*Please,* Alberto!'

I tried to grab his arm, but he shook me off. I knew where he was heading as he stormed from the apartment, and a wave of shame and panic crashed over me. My friend had the gun now, and I had nothing. Not even my pride.

'Open this door.' Alberto was standing outside my apartment, looking strangely calm as he waited for me to let him in. Keeping up had been a struggle, but somehow it felt like I was under orders now. I had barely twisted the key full circle before my friend burst in so forcefully the door slammed back against the inside wall.

'What the hell is this?' Jairo was still at the table. He didn't leave his seat to confront him, however, but to back away. My uncle had yet to hang the curtain again, which gave him a clear view of Alberto advancing on him with the gun in his hand. 'Jesus Christ!' He ripped off his glasses, as if they had just fogged on him. Tell me that isn't real!'

'Sit down.'

Ignoring the request, and panicked by this locomotive coming across the room, Jairo grabbed the roll of parcel tape and flung it at him. The roll hit Alberto in the face, but it was my uncle who shrank away as if he had taken the blow himself.

'Let's talk this through sensibly. Put the gun down, my friend. I'm begging you!'

'Yeah? Begging is all you're good for, little man.'

By now my uncle had backed into the corner beside the window. He was clawing at the wall, looking for any way out. If Alberto was here to scare him some, he had done his job already.

'Please, Sonny,' he cried, appealing to me now. 'I'm sorry for what happened last night, really I am. I was a little drunk and I will never forgive myself, but please don't let it come to this. *Please!*'

Once again my uncle's chest got the better of him, and he broke into a volley of coughs that sounded like sobbing. Alberto went closer and put a hand on his shoulder.

'Calm down,' he ordered, and promptly slipped the muzzle of the gun inside his mouth. Immediately, my uncle stopped coughing and started whimpering instead. Just relax, Jairo, do you hear? Don't cry. Don't let yourself down. Be cool.'

'Alberto, cool it yourself!' I wanted to haul him away, but it was plain that nothing would stop him now.

'Chew on it,' he suggested quietly, like this was a medicine. 'That's right. Yeah. Now we understand each other.'

I was standing beside the curtains, afraid I might collapse all over again. Jairo looked at me with eyes wide and white, and began to sink to the floor. I realised Alberto was guiding him down, putting pressure on the gun until he had him on his back.

There, he cocked the hammer, said: 'You're probably wondering if I can use this, huh?'

'Oh God, no.' I began shaking my head. 'Brother, please don't.'

'Let me tell you,' he went on, 'I had some serious doubts myself, but they made my first hit easy for me. The guy I had to cap was strapped to a fence, all beat up and spread out like a chicken. You know what they did to him next, Jairo?' He paused, and with his free hand traced a finger across his throat. 'They sliced him. Man, they went from ear to ear. I watched the whole thing, didn't see I had a choice, even when they pulled his tongue down through the wound so it's hanging out like a necktie. I had no idea something like that could be done. I didn't understand how anyone could even think of such a thing! So, I'm looking at this poor guy as he suffocates on himself. He's trying to scream but it just makes the blood bubble . . . and that's when they told me to whack him.'

This was Alberto we were listening to here. My best friend from way back, telling us the story in such detail I wondered if this was the first time he had ever put it into words. It felt like we were hearing some kind of unbearable confession, something you wouldn't even dare reveal to a priest.

Alberto glanced over his shoulder, said, 'Sonny, you have to understand I didn't *want* to cap the poor guy. I didn't want to kill *anyone*. But the way they had got him already, it was the kindest thing to do. He was dying there, a slow, humiliating death, right in front of all these people.'

'For the love of Christ, Alberto!' I dropped my hands and spread them, still dealing with the most immediate horror here. 'Take the gun out of his mouth.'

Alberto looked back at Jairo, and appeared to take a second to remember why my uncle was down there on the floor, sucking on a gun. He sighed to himself, tipped his head to one side and said: 'I was putting him out of his misery, that's all. I was doing the right thing, wasn't I?'

This time he really was seeking some kind of assurance, his voice sounding more tightly strung than ever. Jairo just carried on looking up at him, his horrified face frozen around that pistol.

'You did what you had to do,' I said at last, struggling to keep it together as I told him what I thought he wanted to hear. My mouth felt bone dry, and I licked my lips before reaching out to touch his elbow. 'But you don't have to do that here.'

Alberto heard me out but he didn't take his eyes from my uncle. I tried to ease him away, my hand guiding him gently backwards. It was the wrong move this time, I realised, for he shook me off and flexed his finger inside the trigger guard. Uncle Jairo began to moan and breathe in spasms, like his lungs had shrunk and he couldn't keep the air inside.

'Ever I'm asked to kill a man now,' Alberto said next. 'I just have to think of my first time. I don't care what the guy has done so wrong to earn the hit. That's none of my business. All I know is that by taking his shitty life away I'll be helping him out somehow.' At last, but without warning, Alberto removed the muzzle from my uncle's mouth. He wiped his brow with his forearm, took a second away with his thoughts. 'So long as I don't get my vest messy,' he said finally, 'my job is done.'

My uncle tried to speak, to utter thanks, but the air he gulped down just overwhelmed him. Alberto watched him fight for breath, then returned to my side. He put his gun hand between my shoulder blades. I could feel it in his grasp as he patted me on the back.

'Don't ever mess with your nephew again, you hear?' Jairo switched his attention to me next, but I couldn't look him in the eye. I just told Alberto we should leave now. For the first time since we had come into the apartment, he did as I asked. I didn't look at my friend as he passed. I found it hurt to breathe once again, even though I'd barely moved, but that was nothing compared to Uncle Jairo. As I turned for the door, I heard him mutter, 'Asshole kids,' which is when Alberto spun back and shot him.

It happened as suddenly as a lightning strike. No pause for thought. No last warning. He just wheeled around in front of me and squeezed off a shot over my shoulder. The report from the gun brought me to my senses: an almighty *snap* that stayed in my ear so the scream that followed sounded like it was coming from another room. I turned back again and saw my uncle wrapped around his left foot. He had blood seeping through his fingers and looked both stricken and astonished.

'You shot me!' he howled, like we couldn't see that for ourselves. 'You really shot me!'

'So maybe I should've aimed higher!' screamed Alberto, his voice breaking up once more. 'We may just be asshole kids to you, Jairo, but what does that matter? We've got the gun! Right now, *I* decide if you live or die, but if I'm honest you don't deserve to be sent any place. You should be here, with Sonny and his mother, repaying them for taking you in.'

Alberto looked at me, shrugged like this was out of his hands now, and said he had to go. I felt like I was one step behind him in every way. I was in a daze, still struggling with the fact that he had raised a pistol to my uncle. That he had actually fired it just seemed so incredible. In this city, gunshots were as common as car horns. I had seen bodies in the street, ringed off with police tape, but this was the first time I ever saw someone get hit. I had never been this involved before, and it blew me away.

'What about the bullet?' I gasped, remembering what Alberto had told me. 'They're keeping count!'

Alberto looked at the gun, and laughed right out of nowhere. It was as startling as the shot itself, and over in a flash, like some devil inside him had momentarily got a grip. I wondered what had gone through his mind when he pulled the trigger, or if he'd even had time to think at all. He turned to me once again, and told me not to worry myself.

'What matters is I didn't waste the shot, Sonny. Now get him to hospital, tell your uncle to say he did it to himself, fooling with a friend.' He stopped there, glared at Jairo if to shut him up, and began to nod at what he was thinking. 'Tell us what happened to you, man. What's your story for the doctors and nurses?'

My uncle glanced up, his cheeks glistening, and his eyes pinched in pain. 'I . . . I can't say . . . What you're asking—'

'*Speak clearly!*' Alberto insisted, playing with him now. 'You're gibbering!'

'I shot myself in the foot!' wailed Jairo. 'I shot myself, *all right?*'

Alberto stood down with the gun, and asked me for the holster. He looked kind of restless now, not just here in my apartment but inside his own skin. Despite the pain, I unbuckled the strap without any help. In fact, I couldn't wait to get it off.

'I'll see you later, brother,' he said, collecting it from me. He nodded at my uncle. 'Are you OK with him?' He waited for me to answer, taking stock of me. I nodded, my teeth gritted tight to stop them from chattering. I could hear my uncle weeping now, and wished my friend would just leave. I loved him as a brother, but now I saw him in a new light. I needed space to take it in. Finally, he moved towards the door, only to stall and reach for his back pocket. 'I was thinking, Sonny maybe you should look after my match ticket, like you did with the piece.' He glanced at my uncle, making sure he remained out of earshot. 'Way I see things, it's one less thing to worry about.'

9

The emergency room at San Vicente de Paul Hospital is a crazy place. People from every *barrio* went there, including their gang members. Looking for a space when we arrived, I half expected a war to break out at any moment. I couldn't work out what was stopping them from killing each other, but for the need to get patched up. Then I figured maybe Jairo was right. Sometimes it was best just to keep your head down and not ask questions.

Luckily, my uncle was seen quickly, mostly because his breathing had got so tight, and with no questions asked about how his foot had been nicked by a bullet.

'Nicked?' he said, sounding like he'd lost once again. 'It's still a *gunshot!*'

Once he had been checked out, we were told to sit in the waiting area and a nurse would call him to dress the wound. Uncle Jairo was still in an almighty mood as I helped him to a bench at the back, but at least time passed quick enough. There was just such a lot going on: all that noise and blood and emotion, so much life and so much death.

My uncle barely had a good word for anyone, except the intern who came over with painkillers. Most of the time he sat there muttering to himself, though his whispers broke up one time and he started sobbing again. It was a bit embarrassing as a lot of people started looking at us, but mostly I felt for Jairo. The way he breathed in pitiful snatches made me think this went down deeper than the shooting, and I tried to comfort him. I put my arm around his shoulders, and that brought him to his senses.

'Don't be a faggot!' He shrugged me away smartly, and scrubbed his cheeks with his shirt-sleeve. 'Haven't you disappointed me enough already, Sonny?'

I felt bad about what had happened, but at least my bones stopped aching after Jairo offered me the extra pill he'd been given in case the pain got any worse. He may have been mad at me, but I guess in the end he also felt responsible for different reasons. The effects were strong, but I didn't complain. It also made it easier for us both to sit together against that hard wall and watch people come and go. We saw a lot of victims in the hour or so we were there, from what could've been muggings and road accidents, stabbings, fist-fights and some bullet wounds more serious than ours. Some walked in, many arrived on stretchers wearing masks and tubes and all sorts.

When a nurse finally called for my uncle I expected him to snap at her for being made to wait so long. Instead, he accepted her apology without complaint, as if being here had opened his eyes to a few things. I stood up to go with him, but he insisted that I stay behind. The nurse invited him to ease into a wheelchair, and he even nodded at me as she wheeled him backwards through the crowds. I figured old Jairo was relieved to be in good hands. I just wished I could have said the same thing for myself.

All alone, in this hot and crowded space, I went back to fretting that the peace simply could not last. I tried hard not to think about it, but there were just too many faces dotted around who looked like they might be packing. It was as if my life no longer had a safety catch, thanks to Alberto, and now I saw danger everywhere. That he had even got his hands on a gun was a big deal for me. To see him pull the trigger was something else. My life had gone on hold when that bullet whistled past my ear, and when it started again things were different. *Everything* had changed. For me, that gun stopped being something to admire, like a toy that everyone wanted, and become a tool that made things happen. Until then, all those days Alberto got called away were just blank spaces. Now I began to fill them with the kind of tale he had shared with us. I would've accused him of cooking up that horror story just to scare my uncle, but he had gone on to shoot him so calmly that it was clear he knew how to handle himself. Thinking back on that moment, I realised Alberto knew what he was going to do before I had even turned the key in the lock, and that left me in awe of him.

Just then I wished I owned a weapon as well. I wanted the confidence it had given him, also the control. I had no regrets about keeping the pistol holstered the night before. Despite being knocked around, I had at least kept my promise to Alberto. Had it belonged to me, I decided, my uncle wouldn't be here in hospital but on a slab in the morgue.

I pressed my head back against the wall, wishing they would hurry up with Jairo. Every time I caught someone's eye it made me brood again, so I studied the overhead fan instead. It cut the air so slow that a layer of dust had settled on each blade. I even considered going outside for some fresh air. I could handle the antiseptic. It smelled good, in fact – strong, clean – but the din in here was making me tense again. I didn't mind the chatter and the arguments, the alarm bells and beepers. What really got to me were the agonising screams coming from a room along one of the corridors.

It was a woman, I felt sure of that, but I had no way of knowing what was going on. At first it just added to the noise, but over the course of half an hour those screams grew louder, more urgent and frightened. One time the door opened for a moment and everyone in the waiting room could clearly hear her begging for this ordeal to be over. People stirred and scratched their necks, keeping themselves out of it, but now I didn't care about attracting attention. I *had* to hop off the bench and take a better look. What I saw was a man dressed up in a pale blue gown, looking like he'd left that room just to breathe again. He was doing his best to keep out of the way of all the doctors and trolleys, but didn't seem to know which way to turn. He was wearing casual clothes underneath, as if he'd arrived here in a hurry, which made me wonder if the guy was about to become a father. It all fell into place for me then, and I tutted to myself for assuming the worst.

Sitting back again, I turned my attention to the reception desk. A kid my age had just run in, and one of the nurses was dealing with him now. She had a kind smile, and crouched so they could speak on a level. The kid was having some trouble understanding her, I think, because eventually she led him through the waiting area as if it would all make sense to him some place else. That's when I realised the screaming had stopped. The hospital was still humming, but no sound stood out against another. I looked towards the corridor, and saw the nurse approaching the guy I had just been watching. He turned, and the boy left the nurse to race into his arms. From what I could see, both were in tears. The nurse kept her distance, but I never found out what was behind it all because my uncle returned just then, with a bandaged foot and a crutch so he didn't have to lean on me any longer.

'Let's get the hell out of here,' he grumbled, once more looking like all this was down to me. Even so, I was only too willing to go home with him.

I left the hospital thinking scenes of birth and death could look just the same. Maybe the man in the corridor really had become a father, or perhaps his son had just lost a mother, a brother or a sister. Either way, I figured we came into this world the same way as we left: kicking and screaming, and with little choice in the matter. I decided that the guy must have stepped out at the final moment, whatever that was all about. It had been too much for me as well, and I was only watching from a distance. Now I knew just how unbearable things could be at the beginning and the end, I vowed to make the most of my life, just like Alberto. It certainly wasn't going to happen in a waiting area, stuck with all these people.

By the time we found the main exit all I wanted to do was get out there and make my mark.

10

Alberto earned himself a tattoo that same day. It was why he'd gone off in such a hurry, I learned, when he found me out on the scrub with the rusty swings. I had been there for a while – avoiding my mother after she went crazy at my uncle and me.

'What do you mean, you shot yourself by accident?' she had demanded to know. 'You need a gun to do that and so help me Jairo, I'll put a hole through your heart myself if I ever find one here.'

My uncle took the rap without complaint, and weirdly I felt some respect for him. We had been through so much that morning, and come out of it with a shared secret. Even so, I didn't want to make it any harder on him, so I left them to bicker and row. It was no day to be outside, however, and the sun had soon driven me from the rooftop. The scrub was really just a broad and uneven cut-through between two blocks in the *barrio*. Like most kids, I often went there when the city started cooking and it became impossible to stay cool in the shadows. Graffiti tags on the back of the buildings told you how many gangs had tried to claim it as their own, so there was always something going on. Lately shacks had begun to appear on the fringes, and I knew it wouldn't be long before it became a block in its own right. This kind of space in the city was hard to find, but then a storm drain ran the length of it that had become an open sewer

over the years. The banks were steep, creating a deep
and narrow channel that often lured dogs to their death.
You only had to dip a stick into the soupy depths to feel
a dead weight down there of some sort. Still, it made a
good sideline for soccer runs, even if most players melted
away when their turn came to fish out the ball.

A frantic match was in progress when I turned up,
but as bits of me had begun to ache again I chose to
watch from the swings on the other side of the drain.
They had been there since before I was born. Whoever
was responsible must have figured we would put up
with anything if it gave us a chance to get away from
the grown-up world for a while. The stink out here was
revolting, even the breeze refused to carry it away, which
forced you to breathe through your mouth. Maybe that's
why Alberto asked what was with the sour face when he
showed me the design that adorned almost the whole of
his back.

'Sonny, I'm relying on you here. I can't see it with my
own eyes.'

'And I can't believe it with mine!' I declared, feeling
shocked to the core for a second time that day. 'Who did
this to you?'

'You make it sound like they held me down against
my will. Man, it was an *honour!* I came clean about
the missing bullet, and the boss said he respected my
honesty. I thought I might be in some trouble, even when
I explained that your uncle deserved to be punished after
what he had done, but you know what? He took it all in
and told the guys what a fine young man I was shaping up
to be. That's when he took me for the tattoo. He arranged

everything up front, kept saying how far I'd come these last weeks, and stayed at my side all the way through.'

The way he went on about this guy, I thought – like it was his father all over again.

'Did it hurt?' I asked, thinking it would've killed me.

'Like all Hell,' he said with a grin, his voice cracking in the excitement, 'but I swear I didn't cry. I held it together until the cab ride home, and just told the driver I was happy.'

'Are you?'

'Sonny,' he said, sounding offended now, 'don't you know what this means?'

I pushed back on the swing to think about it. 'Let me see it again,' I said finally. Alberto slipped the shirt down to his elbows and turned for a second inspection. Once more, I found myself looking at the two grand black outlines on his back. Each started from a point midway up his spine, fanned to his shoulder blades and then swept down to his waist.

'Angel wings,' I said, just as I had the first time. Then, I had assumed someone had taken a marker pen to him. Now I looked again, I saw the skin was raw like sunburn. It looked painful, especially where the holster strap crossed over, but Alberto seemed numb to any pain. 'Oh boy,' I declared, 'this is gonna *kill* your Mamá.'

'Which is why I bought myself the shirt.' Alberto came round proudly and buttoned himself back into it. 'She won't know,' he said, and tried to drop his voice a notch, 'less some fool tells her.'

'Get real! You can hide it for a week maybe, but what about the rest of your life?' I looked up from my seat on the swing, expecting some kind of explanation, but all he did was shrug.

For the first time ever, we had nothing to say to each other. I sensed Alberto felt as awkward as I did, because we both turned our attention to the soccer on the strip opposite. The last thing I wanted was to talk about what had happened at the apartment. Alberto appeared to have moved on like it was no big deal, and I didn't want him thinking I was still shaken. The gun, and now this tattoo, was turning my friend into a stranger to me. I had sometimes seen other boys floating around the *barrio* with black wings like his – always folded in the same way, as if primed to spread wide. Whatever was going on in Alberto's life, there was no way on earth I could say how much I envied him.

'Let's play some football,' he suggested next, and shook out his limbs like he was busting to get going. 'What do you say, Sonny? I feel like I could *fly* with the ball now I got these on my back.'

'Nah.' I patted my ribs. 'Everything hurts when I move. I'll be fine real soon, but I should take it easy for now. I want to be in good shape for the big match, even if we are just watching it.'

Alberto said that was a damn shame, and fished around in his jeans pocket.

'Still got my ticket?' he asked, and I said sure. Then he came back with a silver wrap from a stick of gum, all folded up at the edges. 'You can finish this, if you like. I don't mind losing it to you.'

'What is it?' I asked, knowing I was holding a powder of some kind.

'Something to make you feel brave,' was all he said, because next thing he winked at me and charged into the match. I watched him leap the drain with both arms flung open, already yelling at the kids on the other side. I smiled to myself, and opened up the wrap. Inside was a small amount of white speckled powder. If this was cocaine, I thought to myself, Alberto would've sold it already. Like a lot of kids, we had grown up believing the cash you could get for this stuff was worth more than the kick. It was a drug for people with too much money, we decided, and you could never have enough of that. Even so, I didn't want to hassle my friend about what I had here in case he laughed at me for not trusting him.

The breeze was stirring it a bit so I cupped the wrap and dabbed some with my fingertip. It was chalky but bitter-tasting, and sort of crackled on my tongue. Then a shout went up from the match, and I looked across to see that Alberto was holding his own already. He had bundled his way into possession and was moving with such a purpose I wondered if those wings of his actually *had* blessed him in some way. He seemed so focused as he took a long, wild shot for goal, and would've seemed invincible to me had it not been for a superhuman keeper. I just wish I had kept my wits about me in the same way. For when I looked down into my hands again, all the powder had been blown away.

11

I began to have some trouble sleeping. It wasn't just the bruises or the memory of what had happened in the apartment that haunted me. What kept me awake most of all was Saturday. The most important fixture of my life had almost arrived, and I could barely wait! I'd lie in my bed, listening to the late night match previews that Jairo kept tuning in to watch. He was a big fan, too, but I didn't dare tell him we owned tickets for the match. He'd only try to steal them from me, most probably when I nodded off. I doubted he would knock me about to get his way ever again. Alberto had guaranteed that for me. I was only sorry that I hadn't sorted it out myself.

Mamá knew that something had gone down between us. Of course she did. Normally, she was never around when things went off, like a row or a fight, but a gunshot was different because of the damage done. The afternoon I returned from the scrub, it was clear that she and Jairo had been arguing about how such a thing could happen – here in her own home and with a gun he couldn't produce. Her eyes were red-rimmed and puffy, despite the make-up she had put on for work, while my uncle had clearly found some peace now he had a prescription for painkillers. He just sat there with his bandaged foot propped on the table, like that was a reason for sympathy not scorn. Still, Mamá did kiss me on both cheeks before leaving for the evening, and said that she would always be proud of me no matter what. She had hugged me, too, so hard I thought I might cry out and give everything away. Over her shoulder I had seen Jairo watching me, and I reckon he was impressed that I kept it together.

We didn't talk much, even after she went out to work. I wasn't very hungry, but I fried up some plantain just to keep my uncle sweet. We ate it with cold rice in front of a documentary about Nacional in the Eighties. There had been lots of footage that showed the stadium packed to full capacity. It was a riot of green and white. Some fans could be seen holding flares that showered coloured sparks over the balconies while everyone just sang and danced and pledged their support to the finest team on earth. I couldn't wait.

'Look closely,' Jairo had said with his mouth full, and gestured at the screen with the fork. 'You might see your old man in the crowd. He never missed a match.'

By Friday, I had forgotten all about my aches and pains. With only one more sleepless night to get through, I was in high spirits when I called for Alberto. There was every chance that he wouldn't be in, I knew that, but then I had come to look forward to the moment when Beatriz answered the door. Even if she was in a rush to get ready for college, she always made time for me.

'Sonny, why don't you just move in with us? I see more of you than my own brother these days.'

What she said made me think of that moment when I had seen more of Beatriz than she ever intended, and all of a sudden I was looking at my shoes. It was only then I realised that she hadn't greeted me with her usual smile.

In fact, she had sounded quite prickly. I felt uneasy, standing there. Too shy to meet her eyes again.

'I'm sorry,' I said, for no particular reason, but once again with her it seemed like the right thing.

'Don't be,' was all she said until she had my full attention. 'I'm sorry, too.' Now I really did feel alarmed. The way she had appealed to me just then, it could only be that Beatriz had Alberto in mind. Over recent weeks she had given up pressing me about him, and I almost thought she was warming to me. I would ask if she knew where he had gone, knowing damn well that she had no idea, and then she would tease me about how I might survive another day in my own company. I didn't mind, even when it became a regular joke for her, because when she laughed she did so with me. It was never at my expense. Looking at her now though, I saw no hint of sunshine in her expression – only storm clouds brewing quietly. I couldn't even bring myself to ask after Alberto this time, because I had a strong sense she had seen right through me.

'I shouldn't be here,' was all I could think to say, and began to retreat from the door.

'Sonny, if you knew something you'd tell me, like you promised, wouldn't you?'

'*Adios*, Beatriz.' I hated myself for doing this, but I just couldn't betray him. Alberto was my brother as much as hers, even if it meant leaving her looking lost in her own home. I took another step back, and that's when her eyes became shiny and wet.

'He's got a gun,' she blurted out.

'*What?*'

'He wears it under his shirt.' She stopped there, swallowed hard but it was too late. Her whole face just melted, and when she tried to speak again her voice broke up. 'He's my little brother, Sonny. Alberto's just a baby!'

'He'll be fine,' I said weakly, and again because I didn't think she had heard me. Beatriz looked so pathetic, trying to get a grip but failing completely. I could feel my own throat tighten, my mouth beginning to twitch, and when I spoke her name no sound came out. I had to do something, but I didn't know what until she dropped her hand from the door and moved towards me.

Only one woman ever hugged me before, though Beatriz felt very different to my mother. I found myself pressed to her chest with her hand in my hair, and my shirt growing damp with tears.

'Oh, Sonny,' I heard her sob. 'What has happened? All night I've been going out of my mind with worry, but I can't confront Alberto. He'd just take off, I know it, and then we'd lose him completely.'

'Beatriz—'

'You have to talk to him, make him see sense. He listens to you.'

'*Stop* this! Leave me be!'

Beatriz pulled away smartly. She looked shocked, like I had just bared my teeth and tried to take a bite out of her throat. I was shaking, still flared up because I had felt so smothered and defenceless. I wiped my cheeks with the heel of my hand, ashamed to be like this in front of her.

'Please help us,' she said, quieter now, one hand reaching out to me, but I'd had enough. I wheeled around and fled for the stairs.

'Alberto can go to Hell!' I yelled when she appealed to me again, and rushed headlong into the street. A car horn blared but I ignored it, and some pigeons scattered from my path. I just had to get away at all costs, if only to escape the feeling that I had woken up in my friend's bad dream.

'So, what's on your mind?' This was Alberto himself, later in the day. I had heard him come into Galán's store and ask after me. I was in the back room, sugaring peanuts and bagging them up. It was the only work on offer at such short notice, but I had taken it anyway. I needed the money. I also knew that Alberto would hunt me down and I wanted him to see me in business. 'Stop that for a moment and talk to me,' he said, trying again. 'I believe there must be some kind of problem because you're here busting your balls for a couple of pesos.'

'It's still work,' I told him, glowering when he helped himself. 'There's no problem here.'

Alberto faced me from the other side of the table. Through the gap in the door behind him, I could see Galán behind his counter. He was hunched over a magazine, reading it so closely I just knew that he hoped to hear every word we said. Still, I needed this job. It was all I had now, and I blamed my friend for this.

'Sonny,' he said next, 'don't play me for a fool here. I heard you had a shouting match with Beatriz.'

'Huh?'

I looked up in surprise. Alberto nodded like it all made sense. Coolly, he tossed a peanut to catch in his mouth, only to miss completely. We both smiled despite ourselves, even if it was just for a moment.

'Everyone knows everybody's business in our block,' he went on, like maybe I had told him this myself one time. 'I hadn't even opened the door before the neighbour came out to give me grief because my big sister and best buddy had been yelling at each other in the hall. People only choose not to hear gunfire, Sonny. You should know that.' This time Alberto was alone in grinning. I saw nothing funny in what had happened to my uncle, though he was right about the bullets. Not one person from our block had breathed a word about the pistol going off in our apartment. Had Alberto stopped short of shooting him, my mother would've known every detail by now. 'Anyway,' he said, still stuck on his earlier question. 'Are you hassling her, Sonny? Just because she's the only girl who gives you the time of day, it doesn't mean you can take liberties. What the hell is going on with you two?'

Alberto was several sizes bigger than Beatriz, and somehow that made it impossible to dodge a direct question. Even if I could cover for him when his sister pressed me for the truth, I couldn't lie to his face. I leaned in over the table, inviting him to come closer.

'You've got to promise you won't freak out if I tell you.'

He said nothing, didn't swear on it as I had hoped, but his expression hardened. It was too late to go quiet now. I glanced around him, just to check Galán wasn't right there at the door waiting for me to speak. If he overheard us talking business, I worried that Alberto's boss would get to hear about it. So when I spoke, I barely moved my lips.

'Beatriz knows you're packing.'

'Oh man! You told her?'

'Me? I didn't breathe a word!'

'But how else could she know?'

'Just keep calm.' I paused to gesture at the door. 'Otherwise people will hear like they do in our block.' Alberto looked uncomfortable. He rubbed his forearm, like the temperature had dropped all of a sudden.

'Who else knows,' he asked. 'Please tell me, not Mamá?'

'It's only a matter of time,' I reasoned with him. 'You can't wear a gun and hope nobody's going to notice. Same with the tattoo.'

'That's *my* business!' he snapped, looking like he didn't care who heard him now, but I told him he was wrong. 'It affects me just as much, Alberto. You can't just leave us behind and expect nothing to change.'

He opened his mouth to attack me, closed it again, and then dropped back by a foot. '*Mierda!* What am I going to do?'

What happened next surprised me as much as Alberto. I set down the sugar shaker, and said: 'Take me with you.'

'What?'

'Next time you get the call, bring me along for the ride.'

'Sonny, what's the boss going to think if he finds out I've been telling people about the stuff I do for him?'

'But you told *me!*' I argued, struggling to keep my voice in check. 'You told me and I have to live with it. I'm the one left to deal with my family and yours, and that's not fair. We're supposed to be equals, after all. You always said we didn't need to be in a gang, but that counts for nothing when you get all the breaks. Please Alberto. You can trust me. I've proved I can look after a gun so I'm asking you from the heart . . . get me some work.'

I was breathless when I finished, I guess because it had all come pouring out. I knew it was what I wanted, but only because I had put it into words at last. This wasn't just about being left behind, I realised now I had spoken. It was about staying friends for life.

Alberto was focused on some imaginary point midway between us. He seemed to be replaying everything I had just said. Finally, he broke off to click the door shut.

'You need money, right? How many times do I have to say it, Sonny? You only have to ask.' He reached for his wallet, and began leafing through the notes inside. I had never seen so much cash before. 'What do you need? Enough to stop packing peanuts for a living? That's fine. Give me a figure, we can go to the mall. Do something nice. All the stores are selling souvenirs for tomorrow's match. We could get ourselves a programme already.'

'I don't want your money,' I snapped. 'And please stop buying me gifts because it doesn't make things better. Alberto, I need to *earn* my way, like you. I want the same kind of options.'

'What options?'

'Alberto,' I scoffed. 'I can't choose what channel to watch on the TV without old Jairo climbing all over my back! You have the right to decide who lives and *dies* for Christ's sake!'

'It isn't a choice,' he said, quietening down now.

'But you can leave!' I argued. 'If you wanted you could use that gun to help start all over again. I don't have that choice. If things go from bad to worse, all I can do is deal with it the best I can.'

'And where do you think I should go, Sonny? Seeing that you got it all worked out?'

I drew breath to remind him about what he had once said about climbing the mountains just to see what was on the other side. It had been his dream, after all, but he was glaring at me now, like he was here to stay.

'Take me on a job,' I said again. 'Then maybe we can move on together, like it should be.'

Alberto looked pained. Deep creases appeared across his brow as he thought things through.

'I have to be at the square in half an hour,' he said finally. 'Things are a little crazy right now. *El Fantasma* says it always kicks off before a big match, I guess because it stirs the blood.'

Without another word, Alberto reached for the door once more and jerked it open. Sure enough, there was Galán listening in from the other side just as I had suspected. Alberto tutted at the storekeeper, who retreated to the counter as if my friend owned the place now.

'What do you think *El Fantasma* will make of me?' I asked them both, because it was clear the storeowner had heard every word.

'What can I say?' Galán touched his chest with his fingertips. 'I already made one introduction.'

Alberto turned back to me, struggling to look upbeat as ever.

'The boss is a big Nacional fan,' he said, and gestured for me to follow him. 'So I guess we're all on the same side.'

'Eh, Sonny!' this was Galán. We turned to find him standing with his palms spread now. 'What about the peanuts?'

'Later,' said Alberto, and glanced at me. 'My brother here never let anyone down yet.'

12

The man with the dead eye was called Manu. For the first time since he pulled up into our lives, I found him looking directly at me. I was standing in front of the fountain, watching from a distance. Alberto had instructed me to keep back when the green Dodge turned into the square, and I did exactly as I was told. My friend had leaned in on the driver's side, talked for ten seconds or so, and then pointed at me. Despite that strange look he had, Manu left me in no doubt that he was scoping me out.

I leaned back against the wall of the fountain, tried to keep cool like I didn't give a damn. A cigarette burned between my fingers, but the truth was I felt too sick to smoke it. The afternoon was still and quiet, but so hot I found it almost hurt to be outside. Shuttered stores and lobby doors surrounded the square, with little green and white flags strung between windows. The place was deserted, closed down for lunch, but most probably in between parties. I tried not to think that it meant I was in the wrong place at the wrong time.

'The name's Sonny,' I muttered to myself, practising what I would say to him. 'I won't let you down.'

The line sounded good to me, just as it did when Alberto had said it in Galán's store. When my friend dipped back to the driver's window again, I hoped maybe he was going to tell him direct. I had no idea what was actually being said, but Alberto bought his hands into the conversation this time and I could hear their voices rising.

'Tell him what I did for you,' I said under my breath. 'Tell him I can be trusted.'

It began to sound bad, the way the pair of them tried to talk over each other. Then Alberto sprung from the conversation and crossed towards me. He kept his head down all the way over, his lips pressed tight together.

'Not today,' was all he said, coming close like he didn't want to be overheard.

'But he took *you!*' I declared. I just wasn't prepared for this. Alberto had been chosen, so why not me?

Manu began to gun the big engine as we spoke. Alberto glanced over his shoulder, and waved like he'd only be a moment more. He didn't seem to realise how much I wanted this. 'Maybe next time,' he said. 'Another day, yeah?'

'I'm ready *now,*' I argued, frantic all of a sudden. I had watched that taxi drive away too many times with Alberto in the back seat. Now I really needed to be there beside him, even if it meant falling out about it first. Maybe I was being selfish and unreasonable, but I couldn't help myself. Manu punched the car horn next, yet I refused to let my friend go. I stood square, my heart racing, and searched his expression for cracks.

'Sonny,' he said eventually, with a tired-sounding sigh. 'I don't make the decisions. I just do what I'm told. Least you can do what you want with your day, even if it doesn't come to much. You don't have to squeeze your eyes shut at any time. You're free.'

'Free from what?'

Alberto didn't have a chance to explain himself, for Manu bellowed his name across the square.

'I'm out of here,' he insisted. 'But hey, it's nearly tomorrow. Who cares about today? When those turnstiles open, I want to be first into the stadium!'

'Alberto, forget about the football for just a second—'

'Swear to me you got my ticket, still.'

'You *know* that already!' I was desperate not to lose out, but angry too. It made me feel even worse about keeping on at him, but this was all about loyalty now. 'I can't face another afternoon on my own,' I confessed. 'All I do these days is wait, and I could be out there making things happen. Talk to him again, Alberto. I'm begging you!'

The sound of a car door snapping open made us both jump. Manu climbed out of the car, and spat furiously at his feet. Alberto seemed totally torn. He looked back at me, and I really thought I had got through this time. Then he clapped me on the shoulder, and all the fight threatened to leave me too.

'Keep those tickets safe, brother of mine,' was what he said. 'I trust you more than anyone.'

'I don't want you to go,' I pleaded, and that stopped him good. My vision began to thicken and swim. I blinked back tears, hoping he wouldn't notice. Manu yelled at Alberto to get his sorry ass into the cab, but this time he ignored him. I swallowed hard, hoping my voice wouldn't crack up on me. 'Alberto, if you're in trouble why don't you stick around? We can make everything like it used to be.'

My friend considered what I had said for what seemed like an age. Even Manu fell quiet, and then returned to his car when Alberto shook his head at me. 'I got wings and a Smith and Wesson,' he said, and made a point of rolling his shoulders before turning for the Dodge. 'Even God can't touch me now.'

I felt ashamed of myself for much of the afternoon. Every time I put myself in Alberto's shoes, I saw a snot-nosed kid in front of me who couldn't take care of himself. It was only when the sun began to set that my anger started rising. People were coming out to begin a great fiesta, but I just didn't feel I could join in, and that's when I started cursing his name again. I even went back to the store to finish bagging the peanuts, only to find Galán had locked up early and pulled down all the shutters. The fireworks began to bloom soon after dark, lifting into the night sky from every direction. It felt like the whole of Medellín was in high spirits except me.

I went home around seven o'clock, found Jairo out cold in front of the box with a Nacional scarf draped round his shoulders. He was slumped back in his seat with his bandaged foot on the table and his mouth wide open. It looked like Alberto had come back and put a bullet down his throat. That he was wheezing made it clear he would still be here to catch the match, while the bottle in front of him warned me to be out of sight when he finally surfaced. Even so, I wondered if I'd feel this numb had I really found him dead in front of his favourite *telenovela*. He didn't stir when I switched it off, and for a while I just sat opposite him, amazed that all the firecrackers and the singing from the streets below couldn't wake him.

It was the eve of the big match, and I had never felt this low in my life. I figured Alberto wouldn't be away for ever, but I refused to call for him. He had let me down badly, I decided, and if our friendship meant anything to him now then he would have to work hard to make up for it. I stretched my feet under the table, and just stared at the bad foot in front of me. I was bored and fed up, which was what persuaded me to take a slug from the bottle. Jairo liked to switch between Colombian beer and cheap brand *aguardiente*. He drank spirits when times were really tough for him, usually this firewater. I never had understood how a drink could help you to forget about your troubles, but the first slug changed all that for me. *Ave Maria!* It practically ignited inside my guts! Even so, it made a change from the joints Alberto had been so keen to roll, so I tipped the bottle to my lips again.

Part of me worried that my uncle would notice that the bottle was lighter when he next poured himself a glass, but slowly that fear faded. I just sat there, sipping every now and then, wishing I could switch him off. He wasn't snoring. That would've been bearable. It was more of a rattle that started too deep down to be in his throat, and I quickly decided that the noise was too much for me.

'Let me play you some Nirvana,' I suggested playfully, aware that I could say anything while he was in this state. 'Actually, just shut up and listen!'

My uncle had finished taping up the beat box, and I was pleased to discover that it still worked OK. The bust-up speaker rattled a bit, but Kurt Cobain made up for that. Jairo didn't twitch even when I turned it up some, so I kicked back with my feet on top of the table just like him. My uncle was totally out of it and remained that way for the next half an hour. He only looked like he might wake up when a knock at the door interrupted our private party. I lunged forward to kill the volume, and that was what disturbed him. It also meant whoever was outside knew that I was in.

It had to be Alberto, I thought to myself, but I was damned if I was going to open up just like that. No way. Now that I knew he would come round I decided he should pay a price for one night only. My uncle groaned and smacked his lips but soon settled back into his slumber. Seconds later, on hearing footsteps return to the stairs, I reached for the bottle again.

'There wouldn't be enough to go round,' I told Jairo, and saluted him with a big swig. The hit lifted me on to my feet, just as a volley of fireworks screamed for the stars outside. It was enough to make my uncle start muttering and mumbling again, and I didn't like the sound of that one bit. Without thinking I turned up the stereo, and amazingly he settled back again. It seemed old Jairo preferred to party alone than celebrate with real people.

There were two rival teams in this city, but from my window it looked like all the fans had come together for a good time. I peered down, hoping to spot some familiar faces I could hang out with, only to see a young woman drift into the street dressed all in white. She seemed divine to my eyes, almost glowing from the inside out as she cut across the crowd. Even before she stopped and turned her pale face up to me, I felt like I had just ignored a visit from one of God's own messengers.

13

I had already made a fool of myself in front of Alberto's sister that day. After the way I had behaved when she broke down about her brother, I didn't think she'd want anything more to do with me. Now it seemed she had been good enough to call at my door, and this was how I behaved! I flinched from the window, unsure if she had seen me, but quickly decided I needed to make up for my stupidity. Alberto had caused us *both* a lot of grief, I thought. Maybe we could help each other.

'*Beatriz!*' I crashed out into the crowded street, and tried to cross just as she had. It wasn't so easy for me, however, and I found myself getting shoved and snarled at and told to take it easy. I turned a couple of times, hoping to catch a glimpse of that flowing white dress she was wearing, but it just made me feel giddy and breathless. What was the point of drinking, I thought, if it made you feel sick as well as sorry? I dug in my heels as best I could, and called her name again. I would've carried on until I heard her voice, but a string of firecrackers went off like a dog fight just behind me. The crowd around it scattered, and I found myself caught up in the push. When I got some space again, I realised I could hear my beat box over all the laughter and the singing. I looked around and spotted our building. Then I saw Jairo at the window. He was leaning out with his drink in one hand, yelling for me to haul my ass back inside. I figured he must've woken as I scrambled to leave the apartment, having left my stereo blazing and the lid off the bottle. I couldn't go back now, at least not without my mother around, and realised that meant I was facing a very long night indeed. Still, with so many people having the time of their lives out here, swapping backslaps, cigarettes and songs, I decided to just go with the flow.

Which was how I wound up outside the stadium when the sun came up next morning, with five thousand pesos in my pocket, a strained wrist and a swollen lip.

The money would buy me a McDonald's meal at most. At any other time, it would've been a stretch, but this had cost me a beating, as well as my appetite. I had nobody else to blame for that, and decided it was time I grew up a bit. After turning my back on the apartment, I had hooked up with some kids from the *barrio*. They were just babies really: eight and nine-year-olds who earned a living selling fake lottery tickets at the traffic lights three blocks south. I even heard they pulled off a carjack some days before, and didn't doubt it. They certainly looked like they could shape up into a gang, with their bandanas and the switchblades that came out when I asked them how they'd persuaded three men from the petroleum company to part with their Chevrolet. The way they acted out the scene made me hoot with laughter, and I wished I had been there to see a dozen oily scraps cram into the car and then bicker about who would do the driving. It was clear to me they lacked a leader, and amid the celebrations I had gone a little wild with them.

'Show us what you're made of,' they had said, and that was how it started. 'We never hung with the brother of a *sicario*.'

What money I went on to make had come out of a purse: the result of a dare gone wrong. I was feeling drunk and headstrong at the time, and keen that they remember me. I didn't have a gun like Alberto, but I wanted the same kind of respect and attention. *Watch me,* I had said, and taken a book of tickets into the traffic. In this city, you drove with the doors locked and never wound down your windows. Unless, of course, you were stuck at the lights and a boy like me was pretending to sell you the winning slip. It had taken a little longer than I hoped, however, and I guess I panicked. The kids had begun to make jokes at my expense. *Shifting tickets is child's play!* That's what they had called across when I made my second sale, so I just went for it: I waited for the next car to stop for me, put my hand up under my shirt, as if reaching for a holster, and made out I was packing a piece. The woman in the driving seat had freaked out completely, which startled me almost as much. I should've fled as soon as she flung her purse at me. Instead, I just stood there with my prize. I was utterly amazed at what I had done, and only came to my senses when some college jocks from the car behind leapt out to her rescue.

The kids had fled into the night just as soon as they saw that I was in trouble. Alberto would never have abandoned me like that. I only had to think of the lesson he taught my uncle to remind me of his courage. He may have walked away when I needed him that afternoon, but nobody had been threatening to squash me into the tarmac at the time. Had my friend been around when those jocks caught up with me, I doubt I would've taken yet another beating. When I finally slipped from their clutches, with my t-shirt torn and my head in a daze, I realised how much I missed him.

Without Alberto, it seemed I would never be anything more than a victim. When I caught up with him, I decided, I would make sure he never left my side again.

He might as well have been with me when I found myself outside the stadium, because nobody tried to shake me down. It had seemed like the only place in this city where I felt at home, even if it was the middle of the night and as dangerous as the jungle. There were plenty of shadowy figures drifting around, also drunks and diehard fans waiting for the ticket office to open the next morning, but nobody paid any attention to the boy with the bloody lip and the distant stare. I guess it helped that I looked robbed already, and I was in no mood to make my presence known. I just took myself to the spot where Alberto and I had knocked so many balls about whenever a match was on, and that's where I settled down. I didn't move when dawn broke, all curled up with my hands under my cheek, and only got to my feet again when the space around me began to shrink. I grew thirsty too, with no escape from the strengthening sun, but I worried that I'd miss my friend if I moved from the crowd. At times I had to shove and push to stay standing, but the crush I was in just melted when the gates finally opened.

Towards kick-off, the space I had claimed was almost my own again when some more kids showed up with a ball. They knocked it about for a bit, and then started their own match when a roar from the stadium marked the real kick-off. Using t-shirts for goalposts, they put in their own ninety minutes with all the passion and guts of the players on the pitch itself. Throughout I just stood there with two tickets in my hand and a heart slowly dying in my chest. I even missed the result, but by then I had finally woken up to what I had lost.

Alberto was gone. I knew that I would never see my blood brother again or discover what had happened to him. That much was clear to me just as soon as he had left me in the square, and maybe it was clear to him too. Perhaps neither of us wanted to face up to that last goodbye, but now the final whistle had blown and I was alone in this city. Old Jairo never had a good word to say about me, even when my mother was around, and I didn't dare think about Beatriz now. With nobody watching over me, my only hope was to own a gun.

I also knew exactly how I could earn one.

The Man

The old Dodge Dart speeds towards the compound, sweeping up dust as it fishtails out of every corner. Sunlight detonates from the windshield every now and then, especially when the car passes over a pothole. The boy in the back seat looks straight ahead, tapping out some imaginary rhythm on his knees. On the final turn, his driver jabs the horn three times –a signal for the guard to open the gate. The Dodge accelerates, forcing the guard to hurry and curse, and then slides to a halt inside using the handbrake only. Manu likes to make an entrance, especially when returning from a job well done.

The compound is made up of a number of single storey buildings, three of which look out on to a courtyard. The walls are whitewashed, with sloping red-tiled roofs and a covered porch. Geraniums hang in pots from the eaves, offering yet more escape from the sun. A group of men are drinking coffee round a table in the shade here, while the two white mastiffs that have been basking on the steps come to life as the car doors swing open. These are attack dogs, with slathering jaws and muscular bodies. When the boy drops out he is almost knocked off his feet, and yet he seems unfazed by the attention.

'Hey, girls, did you think I wasn't coming back?' He ruffles one dog behind the ears, and then grabs the other

99

in a headlock. He's no match for these beasts, should they choose to turn on him, but the pistol grip sticking out of his pants suggests he knows how to handle himself. If anything, he looks pleased to have found some playmates at last, and relieved to be out in the fresh air again. The comedown from the injection Manu had given him was bad enough. It helped him see a job through, but as the calming effects wore off so the bad guts and the twitchy feet kicked in, not to mention the ringing ears – even from a single shot. The last thing he wants after a hit is to be cooped up in a car that reeks of freshener. What he really needs is a little space to work off the churn and slosh going on inside his stomach. That'll come later, however. First he has to speak to the individual waiting for him inside the building. El Fantasma only left his quarters when it was absolutely necessary, which boiled down to business and soccer.

The boy stops fooling with the dogs and looks around for Manu, his driver these last few weeks. He's with the others now, pouring himself a coffee and talking with a cigarette pinched between his lips.

'Hey,' the boy calls out to him. 'Where's my picture?'

'Passenger seat.' Manu grins at one of the men. 'I'm thinking I shall become a portrait photographer.'

The boy finds what he's looking for: a Polaroid taken by his driver when he collected him from the scene. It was all part of the deal. The proof before he got paid, maybe something more. He holds the picture in the palm of his hand, buckling it slightly, and wonders if the widow will clean and press the suit her husband died in. Every time he hopes to avoid making a mess, but it isn't easy. At his height, and at such close range, it's hard to carry out a simple *headshot. Knowing the boss as he does, it means that season ticket he's been promised as a bonus might just have to wait.*

'Adios, senor,' *he whispers, and braces himself for an audience with* El Fantasma. *'Alberto will take care of you now.'*

14

I never went looking for the work. Manu claims I couldn't wait to talk to him, but if that's true then why did I keep seeing his cab around the *barrio?* In the week that followed Alberto's disappearance, I would look over my shoulder and there it was – like a dog who wouldn't go home.

'Still ready to ride, huh?' This was the first thing he said when I finally turned and talked to him. I nodded, said I understood. 'What's your name, brother?'

'Sonny,' I told him.

'Sounds like Shorty.' He picked at his teeth, gave up waiting for me to smile and invited me to get in.

I felt no fear, that day. As we swept through narrow streets and market squares, I realised that I hadn't actually felt much at all since the big match. I'd spent my time steering clear of people and places that might have made me cry.

Sometimes it seemed as if everyone in my building and *barrio* was grieving for Alberto, which made it hard for me to be alone. I thought about him constantly, of course. I would see things through his eyes, and was aware of the empty space at my side wherever I went, but that was all. I didn't howl or lose any sleep, and when the police came to ask some questions I just shrugged like they expected.

It was only when I climbed into the cab that I stopped feeling so numb. By the time we pulled up outside a warehouse on the south side, I felt almost human again. Manu didn't believe me when I said I knew what was expected of me. It turned out he was right, because he reached for a box in his glove compartment and insisted I take a jab.

'You kids can get a little excitable at times,' he explained, and picked out the syringe with his fingers. I watched him squeeze a little fluid from the needle. 'What you have to understand is that it isn't just for your own good, but all the grown-ups depending on you. Now, lean forward, Sonny. Give me your arm, that's it. All you have to do is think of your special place.'

'I haven't got one.'

'Everyone has a special place,' he assured me, like I only had to think a little harder. At the same time, he wrapped an old leather shoelace around my arm and instructed me to hold it with my free hand.

'Does it have to be an injection?' I asked, knowing what was coming.

'The hit is instant, Shorty. Trust me, it's worth it because you don't want to go in there with any doubts.'

I sensed goosebumps rising when Manu turned my arm, and wondered if there was anything more that Alberto hadn't told me. I made myself watch what he was doing, from the moment the needle seemed to melt into my skin. I didn't think it would look good if I closed my eyes or glanced away. By the time he had finished with the jab, however, I felt no need to even pretend that I was ready. My skin had stopped prickling and my thoughts no longer raced ahead of me. I had come here for a reason, and now I was locked and loaded. Manu opened the car door for me, and I stepped out on to the parking lot. It was bright outside, but I didn't squint or shield my eyes. In fact, I was struck by how crystal clear the sky seemed.

'It's a beautiful day,' I said, looking up and around, but Manu didn't reply. I could hear screams before we had found the door, not that it rattled me one bit. I knew exactly what I would find inside – a group of guys surrounding some poor fool. This one had been bound by the wrists to an upturned pallet. The warehouse was big and empty and broken-up inside. There were containers strewn everywhere, broken glass and bird shit underfoot.

'Where's the piece?' I asked, breaking the silence when they turned to take a look at me. I didn't meet their eyes or ask again, just stared at the guy I was here to hit. He was much older than I expected: thinning grey hair and an earring that didn't look right on him. His mouth had been stuffed with an oily cloth, and it was clear that he'd been badly beaten. I stared at him and he looked right back at me, and I saw that we had an understanding. Out of respect, I didn't break that connection even when I felt the grip come into my hand.

'Don't fail me,' Manu breathed into my ear. 'I'll kill you myself if you screw this up.'

I had a gun, at last. I held it loose beside me, watched one of the guys pick up a hacksaw from a workbench behind him.

'What's your name, kid?' he asked.

'Shorty,' said Manu, before I could speak. 'It's his first.'

'Well, Shorty, I got a tradition here I want you to see. Let me show you how we tie a Colombian neckerchief.'

The other guys chuckled nervously and made some space for him, and that's when I opened fire on the man he was about to cut.

Without blinking, I watched plugs of bloody flesh and fabric pop from his chest. He bucked and twitched and grimaced with every hit, but I carried on squeezing the trigger until the magazine ran out of bullets. I didn't need to see what my friend had witnessed before me. I just wanted to get the job done, and save us all some time and dignity.

The noise from each gunshot was tremendous, but it was the final one that seemed to slam around the warehouse for an age. Nobody said a word when I dropped my shooting arm, though what I had done left me breathless. Alberto might've left me behind, but this proved I could keep going without him – and do so with my head held high. The old man hung from the pallet like his bones had turned to twigs, but everyone was looking at *me*.

'You're enthusiastic. I like that in my *sicarios*. Maybe you were a little generous with the bullets, but the sucker had it coming.' *El Fantasma* was about the same age as my first hit, though he wore white sneakers with a suit jacket and jeans and that made him look much younger. 'For six months that greedy jackal has been running to the cops about every move I make. Lucky I got friends on the force, huh?' I nodded when he looked at me, tried to stand still. *El Fantasma* had a round face, with curly dark hair that reached the collar. He was perched on the front of his big wooden desk, a signed photograph of the Nacional squad in a frame behind him, a single skin joint between his fingers. I would be taken to meet him at his compound after each job and didn't once see him without a private little reefer between his knuckles. Still, his thoughts never seemed clouded and his eyes were always clear. I heard he didn't touch any other drug, even though his business was to supply others in bulk, but it paid not to ask those kind of questions. One thing I was sure about: he could count out money with the same grace and speed as a card player dealing from a deck. 'Here,' he said next, and snapped out ten notes from a money clip. 'Put this in your pocket and keep it somewhere safe. There are thieves in the city, don't you know?'

He chuckled to himself as I folded it away, but then suddenly his mood changed and he told me to hand over the gun.

'Pardon me?'

It was the first time I had felt afraid, but I refused to let it get the better of me. I just did as I had been asked. *El Fantasma* returned to the seat behind his desk and placed the weapon on the table. Then he unlocked the drawer and took out a box of bullets.

'I have a feeling you'll be getting through plenty of these,' he said, filling the magazine. Just make sure they end up in the right place, Shorty. I know you and me have some history, but what can I say about that? If people flout the rules on the pitch, they got to expect a red card, am I right?'

'Yes, sir.'

'Who do you support?'

I looked up at the photo in the frame. 'Same as you.'

'Amen to that. What position do you play? I'm thinking a little firebrand like you should feed in from the wing.'

'I play anywhere I'm needed,' I told him.

He nodded like he understood what I was saying and pushed the gun across the table.

'Welcome to the team,' he finished with a wink, and from that moment on I set out to become his star player. I saw it as my duty – not just to myself or the friend I had lost, but to the people who mattered to me. If I could help to pay their way, I decided, I would be offering hope.

With some money in my pocket at last, I returned to the *barrio* that afternoon and headed for the one apartment I had avoided since Alberto went missing. I did wonder if I could see it through. My stomach was beginning to feel a little loose, and my mouth tasted like I'd been sucking on a peso. I knew from having spent so much time with my friend that this was down to the jab. I just hoped the calming effects hadn't worn off completely

'Who's there?' Beatriz sounded different from behind the door, scared almost, but that changed when I said my name.

'Go away. Don't come here any more.'

'Please. I have something for you.'

'It's too late,' I heard her say. 'Leave us in peace, Sonny.'

Beatriz was speaking for her mother here, too. I knew this because when it became clear that her son would not be coming home she had retreated from the world around. Several times I had decided that I needed to face Alberto's family, that I owed them kind words at least. I would raise my hand to the door, but always stopped short of knocking. Often it was the sound of weeping that persuaded me to walk away, but mostly it was me. I simply hadn't been able to face his only sister, and went out of my way to avoid her more than anyone else I knew. Until, that is, I had something I could offer to make up for their loss.

'Beatriz,' I said, trying again, and made sure the pistol in my waistband was well hidden. 'I will not leave until you open up.'

'Are you deaf as well as dumb? We don't want any more trouble. We never wanted any of this in the first place. Now we don't even have a body to bury, Sonny. We can't grieve, but we have to move on.'

'I miss you!' What I said came from the heart, and silenced the voice behind the door. 'I miss Alberto, too, but we're still here, aren't we?'

That was when I heard the bolt shoot back. The door opened up, and there she was: older than I remembered, sadder too. She had dark rings under her eyes and appeared to have lost some weight.

'Go home, Sonny.'

Beatriz was wearing the same white dress I had seen her in on the eve of the big match, but it didn't look so special in this light. I could hear another person in the apartment. For a second I expected to see her brother spring out of nowhere, looking loaded up on pastry cake and ready to seize the day. Instead, I caught sight of his mother, just a shadow behind a screen. I didn't know what to say. All I could do was press a fistful of money into Beatriz's hands: half of what I had earned, but enough to make her gasp.

'What is this? Oh, Sonny. Not you, too?'

Maybe she had been close to tears when I called, because her eyes welled before I could explain that I knew what I was doing. She looked at me in disbelief, tried to return my gift, but I just stepped away with my palms raised.

'Take it,' I said. 'It's the best I can do.'

I could see that she was touched. There was nothing I could've said about her loss that would come close to this, and so when she flung the notes in my face it knocked what life I had left right out of me.

'The best thing you can do is *disappear!*' she exploded. 'Get out of our lives, idiot! Leave us in peace!'

15

My mother was the last person I had wanted to face that day. It was only when I saw her that I realised why. I walked into the apartment, expecting grief from Jairo, and my guard just fell away. I thought I might start crying from shock or sheer relief, so I swallowed hard and took some deep breaths.

'Look at you,' she said, from her seat at the table. 'My boy.'

Normally, I would come in to find my uncle in the same place, looking like *I* was the last person *he* wanted to see. The apartment seemed so peaceful without him: filled with light and fresh air. She stood to greet me, drawing back the chair without making a sound. It wasn't just the pistol under my shirt that stopped me from walking into her arms. If she hugged me now, I thought, I might just tell her everything.

'Where is he?' I asked, getting a grip once more. I glanced behind the curtain, but he wasn't napping in the bed. For a second I wondered if the old bastard had died. It explained the rosary beads I noticed she was clutching. 'What's wrong?'

'You're here,' she said. 'It's all that matters.'

Mamá's voice sounded thick and dreamy, like she was speaking to a spirit and not her own son. She didn't blink enough to be natural, either, but then she'd been this way since she learned about Alberto. When she found out,

110

I had expected her to join my uncle and scream at me. Instead, she disappeared for an hour, and came home like she'd lost her soul in the streets. She would weep to herself without warning, and often drifted into thoughts so deeply that Jairo took to shaking her out of herself. He kept on at her about the fact that the world didn't stop turning just because one dumb kid had wasted his life, and that unless she shook off this depression and started paying the rent we would all be better off dead. I hadn't blamed her when she went out to work and didn't come home for two nights, even if it meant Jairo found something else to grizzle about.

After all the hassle my uncle gave us, I had been more than ready to speak to Manu. At the very least, it got me out of the apartment and earning a living. I reached for my pocket once more, and showed my mother the money I had made. Having just tried to give Beatriz her half, I was prepared for the worst. So I pressed it into her hands now, said a silent prayer that she wouldn't surface from her thoughts too quick, and told her everything would be just fine.

'It's all yours, Mamá. If Jairo tries to claim it for himself, you tell me.'

She looked up from the money, not even a hint of surprise behind the glaze. Her lips were moving some, but no words came out this time, so I rocked on to my toes to kiss her on the cheek and told her I had to be some place. I just didn't want to be around when my uncle came home.

'Where are you going?' I heard her say, as I turned to leave.

'Nowhere special.'

'Will you be home again?' The way she asked me this, I could've been the adult leaving a child behind. Still, she sounded concerned this time, and I realised I had to get away quick. '*Sonny?*' I darted out into the hallway. In her state, I thought, she might just forget all about me as soon as I disappeared. I swung on to the stairs and saw her follow me out to the rail with the money in one hand and her rosary in the other. She called out how she loved me, but it didn't sound all there. Still, I left knowing where I wanted to be.

The first thing I did when I arrived was talk to Alberto. I leaned forward in the pew at the back with my hands clasped tightly together, and tried very hard not to let go of myself. It felt quite natural to me, being inside a church. In Medellín there was always one just a block away, but few like this with doors open night and day. Mostly they were padlocked shut, but this place had been plundered so many times there was nothing left to protect. It meant when the faithful filed out after each service, everyone else crept in. As a child, I used to come here with my uncle. The trouble was his turn in the confessional often went on for an age. As a result, I had grown up thinking church was a place to misbehave when the priest wasn't looking, but all that seemed behind me now.

The peace in here was unreal. It could've been a world away from the surrounding city. Candles flickered in front of a plywood altar, also at the back where the Fallen Christ once hung, and the air was laced with incense and dope. In the pew across from me, several boys were sharing a joint and talking in hushed whispers. I had noticed one of them had black-feathered wingtips peeping from his vest, but that just reminded me to mind my own business. I had come in feeling restless and anxious to find some hash myself, but once I'd settled down all the tension seemed to ease. I didn't think it was right to talk to God, after what I had done, but spoke to my friend at length. I told him about the hit and asked him what he thought of me now. I told him I would take care of his family, even if Beatriz needed a bit of time before she realised how much she meant to me. I was going to ask how he felt about that as well, but a tap on my shoulder made me gasp and reach for my gun.

'Easy, man!' said the boy who had disturbed me, the one with the wings and the nub of a joint I realised he had come to offer. He backed away, glaring at me savagely. 'You were looking a little lonely, is all.'

16

I felt refreshed when I left, and ready to face the streets again. I hadn't made any friends, but I did feel I'd spent some time with an old one. I guess that's why I kept going back. Every time I took ride in the taxi, I'd ask Manu to drop me off outside the church. It was kind of hard, spending so much time with my thoughts, but I preferred being there than up on the rooftop. I had returned to our old haunt a couple of times, but it felt like something was missing. Jairo had laid claim to my beat box, which meant I couldn't even bring Kurt for company, and slowly I grew to prefer the pew.

Alberto would've been appalled. In his time he believed in God. I just doubted God could really believe in us any more, though I was drawn to hole out in His house.

In some ways, the hits became easier. I didn't have to think, was why. I just did what I was told each time and got paid for it. Nobody ever went into much detail about what these people had done so wrong, and I didn't ask. On some jobs, I wouldn't have to fire my gun at all. I would walk into an office, bar or lock-up, show it to whoever Manu had pointed out to me, and invite them to step outside. People rarely kicked up a fight, or tried to flee when they looked down into the muzzle. Some would give me a cold, hard stare before their heads were hooded, but mostly they seemed ready for me and the big silver jeep that often came to collect them. Manu never let on where they were taken or why they had to travel in the trunk. Privately, I wished I could've been allowed to finish things before they found out for themselves.

'I know every street, building and back alley in Medellín,' he said. 'But there are some places best left to the imagination.'

I also saw a lot of bodies, but not all my own work. We travelled to trail ends of the city where killing was so commonplace that corpses lay in the street like sacks of refuse. I never dwelled on how these people died, but I thought a lot about the afterlife. Alberto had made it, and I knew that one day I would follow – as we all would. So long as I had provided for the people I left behind, I would be ready to catch up with my friend.

All through this time, I grew more and more fond of my *barrio*: not just the church but also the streets where I grew up, the noises and faces familiar to me. I think it was the jabs that made me feel this way. To begin with they helped me avoid disappointing the boss, but gradually I felt less keyed up about pulling the trigger. I didn't *need* calming, which meant when Manu sunk that needle into my arm I'd simply feel washed out. All I ever wanted to do afterwards was head home, but first Manu would insist on driving by to take a photograph. We needed it as proof for *El Fantasma,* and we had to see him so I could pick up my pay. Each time he would study the evidence, quietly dragging on his toothpick joint as if he couldn't breathe without it. I could never be sure if he was thinking about his victims or the future without them, but whatever weighed on his mind it went down deep. Then, when he had finished with his thoughts, I'd watch him toss the picture on to his desk like it meant nothing to him any more. Once, he overshot the desk completely. I reached down to pick it up, came back to find he'd lifted his hands in surrender.

'Keep it,' he suggested. 'As a kid, I loved collecting.'

'Thank you but no,' I replied, and placed it on the desk. 'I only collect banknotes.'

That had made him roar with laughter. He even called in his guard so he could repeat what I said, though I hadn't meant to be funny. The money was the only reason I kept coming back. It meant after church I could return to the apartment block and push an envelope under Beatriz's door. With every delivery, I braced myself for her to slice it back into the hallway. I would wait for a minute or more, until I felt certain it would not come back. She would face me one day. I felt sure. It was just a question of time.

And when she finally opened that door, I would be ready.

I missed her brother like mad. I missed his lust for life. Everything seemed so flat without Alberto, but when it came to Beatriz I still had some hope. I'd grown up fast since he'd gone, and really believed that one day soon she might treat me as an equal. The age gap meant nothing to me any more. After all the things I had seen and done lately, I felt older than the years I had lived. I began to think that with age came a sadness that was hard to shake, and so I decided to treat myself. Alberto had once done the same thing to keep his spirits up, and so I went to the mall he liked the most. I wanted Beatriz to find me at my best. I also wanted to hear music again.

The first thing I bought was a personal stereo player, then a holster for my gun and a nice white t-shirt to cover it up. My uncle could lust after the player as much as he liked. From now on, if he tried to shake me down he'd be in for a nasty surprise. The shirt was a little on the big side maybe, even if it was a size Small, but there was no way now that I could be seen wearing kids' clothes.

I didn't worry about wearing my headphones in the street. I had no fear of being robbed any more, after all. The little kids and the market traders made sure they recognised me, Galán would nod if I passed his store and even Jairo began to treat me better. Sometimes, he would offer me a drink whenever I returned home, or let me smoke at the window. I knew he was wise to the money I had given my mother because all of a sudden he could afford quality beers, and whisky instead of *aguardiente*. Still, my uncle was no fool. Whenever I did agree to sit with him, if only for a tomato juice, his eyes would dart to my gun. Unlike Alberto, I didn't see much point in trying to hide it. I always holstered it away from Mamá, even before she started breaking down on me, but it did Jairo some good to see the grip peeking from my waistband.

'I appreciate what you've done for your mother,' he whispered once, leaning in across the table even though we were alone. 'Give her time, she'll see what a sacrifice you're making.'

Old Jairo knew better than to demand I pay him directly, just as I knew not to tell him that only half the money was coming into this apartment. He wanted to know who was employing me, of course, but my silence on that subject seemed to tell my uncle enough. It certainly persuaded him to defend me when it all became too much for Mamá, though nothing would stop them from flaring up. I would take off from the apartment, and by the time I reached the street it sounded like I had started a war.

If Manu was nothing more than my driver and minder, *El Fantasma* became like a manager to me. We'd settle up, only for him to draw me into a debate about Nacional's form or insist I try out on the pitch opposite the compound. None of his people told me how he hated to lose, but when I stole the ball from under his feet he was first to break the silence with applause. He could be just as supportive in family matters, too, and seemed pained when I told him how I lived with so much unrest.

It was Manu who told me that *El Fantasma* had lost a wife and young son in a bomb blast some years earlier. He said it had scarred the boss so deeply that he never spoke about it, so I felt privileged when I collected my money after taking out some bigmouth businessman one day and he thanked me for banishing some demons.

'The guy you just capped,' he explained, and crushed the Polaroid in one fist. 'His cousin murdered two people dearest to my heart. Your finish could still use some work, Shorty, but I gotta say you're close to earning that season ticket.'

I felt uneasy when he took out his money clip, having figured he was talking about his family. *El Fantasma* owed me for the hit, but now it seemed wrong somehow. 'You must miss them very much,' was all I could think to say, and he looked at me in surprise. At first I thought he was going to get cross with me for intruding. Instead, he smiled to himself and started counting out the notes.

'The day that bomb exploded,' he said eventually. 'I swore I would track down the sonofabitch responsible and punish every single member of their family. Men, women, children, they all die.'

The way he said this, it was like we were talking about nothing more than horseflies. 'Was it meant for you?' I asked.

'There are many ways to kill someone before you take their life.' He stopped there for a moment, and looked at the money in his hand. 'I used to believe this business was my family's passport out of here. Now the business is all I have, and I'm stronger for it. I don't feel remorse or pity any more, and nor do I have any hopes for the future. It's the only way to survive in this life, Sonny. You follow your team with all your heart but accept that you just can't win all the time.'

El Fantasma insisted I take what I had earned, clearly brooding some because when his bodyguard walked in without knocking he bawled him out on the spot. The guy was built like a superhero, which made the panic in his face so alarming. 'Some cops are at the gate,' he said breathlessly. 'Detectives with a warrant.'

'*What?* Why did we not know about this?'

'*Senor,* how clean are we here?' The guard's eyes shifted to me, but I didn't know what to say. I just stuffed the money into the pocket of my jeans.

'You have to go,' said *El Fantasma* and grabbed the screwed-up Polaroid from the desk. 'Take this with you, and get out of here.'

'With Manu?' I had left my driver in the courtyard, where I figured he was probably involved with the face-off with the cops.

'*Vanish!*' The order barely rose above a whisper, but there was fury there, so I just took the picture and ran.

17

I left the building through the kitchens, and just kept my head down outside. Guards and staff were everywhere, crossing a grass quad with boxes and documents. All of them were heading in different directions, and in a hurry too. Nobody paid any attention to me, though my heart picked up the pace when a knot of cops came around the corner. I doubled-back as they took stock of the chaos that had broken out this side, and sprinted for a sidewall. Frantically I scrambled to get over and away, scraping my knee as I dropped on to the road, but nobody followed or fired a warning shot. If that was a police raid, I thought, someone had clearly paid to make the cops move in slow motion.

I was on the wrong side of the city from home, but I figured the walk would burn up the remains of the jab. It also left me with plenty of time to brood about what had happened. In seconds, *El Fantasma* had gone from treating me like an equal to a little kid, and I didn't like it. I felt angry and ashamed as I trudged through block after block. I also felt out of my depth. I was so far from my *barrio* that some of the street names were totally new to me. Only the mountain ridges were familiar, and helped to guide me in the right direction, but it didn't make me feel any safer.

Even with a loaded gun, I worried I might be jumped. I knew I couldn't risk hailing a cab out here, in case I wound up in the trunk with a hood over my head. I'd learned from Manu that many drivers did his kind of sideline work, taking jobs as wheelmen and messengers. It meant if I raised my hand and a driver for a rival boss recognised my face, I might arrive home bit by little bit until someone paid my ransom. Manu was the only driver I trusted. Locked inside his car, I could go to any quarter of this city and feel protected from the world. Things were different out on the streets. Every passer-by seemed to shoot me a glance, more so as twilight settled, and when squad cars began howling in the hills I immediately assumed they were coming for me. It forced me to keep my head down, even when the buildings became familiar and my apartment block came into view. I crossed the street, thankful that I'd made it just as night fell. A figure stepped out of the lobby just then, laughing with someone behind her. She turned to see where she was going, and then covered her mouth when she saw me.

'Beatriz!' I was just as surprised, but also overjoyed. 'My God, it's good to see you.'

'Sonny, hello.'

She looked amazing, a real bombshell: from her shiny red shoes to the dress that fitted just perfect. She'd fixed up her hair with pins as well, and swapped her college books for a bouquet of flowers. This wasn't a grieving sister I saw before me, but the girl I had been waiting for all this time. As I struggled for something to say, I decided that *El Fantasma* had to be wrong. You couldn't live without hope. You just couldn't.

'It's so good to see you again,' I said, beaming still, but all she did was turn and this guy appeared right behind

her. He was older than me, also Beatriz, and had a sandy
flop of hair cut short over the ears. I knew straight away
that he couldn't be from round here. He was wearing a
pressed shirt with a jumper thrown over his shoulders,
even a mobile phone clipped to his belt. A college jock,
I was sure of it.

'Sonny, this is Juan Mario Uribe. We're studying the
same course. Sonny is a neighbour.' That was how she
introduced me, which stung all the more.

'Pleased to meet you, Sonny.' He held out his hand, but
I ignored it. All I could do was look at Beatriz and what
she had become. The dress and the shoes were brand
new, and we both knew how she had afforded them. I
wanted her to look me in the eyes, if only to see if there
was any shame, but she refused me even that.

'We should go,' said Juan Mario, and glared at me as
he slipped his hand around her waist.

The guy was a jerk. I could've finished him without
thinking, had it not been for Beatriz and the bullet it
would cost me. So instead I stepped to one side, lost
inside myself. I felt betrayed, but only by what I saw
now as a dumb dream. I should've listened to Alberto all
along. What would someone like Beatriz see in a stupid
kid like me? I had nothing to offer, but for the money in
my pocket, and suddenly that seemed worthless.

'Sonny?'

I looked over my shoulder, saw Beatriz facing me.
Juan Mario was looming over her, clearly annoyed that
she had stopped again.

'You helped me to move on,' she said.

'How? By staying away or by paying for a new outfit?'

'Both, in a way.'

I was mad with Beatriz, and wanted her to know it. What she had just said left her blushing, but it also made me think. I hadn't ever considered what she might do with the money. I was trying to make things better. Maybe her brother had hoped to do that with all the gifts he had given me. All I knew now was that Beatriz had a life ahead of her, no matter what happened to me. I blinked until I saw her again, smiled and raised my hand.

'Take care of yourself,' I said, but she didn't smile back.

'I saw your uncle this afternoon, Sonny. I told him how grateful I was to you for thinking of my mother and I, but he agreed you had to stop the hand-outs now and put your own family first.'

'You spoke to Jairo?' I began to bristle again, but not because of her new boyfriend or the fact that this was beginning to sound like a lecture.

'Let *him* take care of *you*,' she suggested. 'We all need help to move on, Sonny. Even if you don't think you need it.'

This time, Juan Mario Uribe succeeded in steering her away from me. I worried some harm might come to them, all dressed up like that in the streets, but figured that was his responsibility. Besides, I had already taken her advice about family to heart, and was rushing up the first-flight of steps.

The door to our apartment eased open just as soon as I tried to slot the key inside the lock. It was dark inside, the blinds shut down, but I left the light off. Instead, I inched in with my gun arm cocked, ready to take out my uncle because this wasn't right. Now that he knew I had kept half the money from him, I figured Jairo should've been here waiting for me. Then, out of the stillness, I heard a single sob.

'Mamá?' I hit the switch, saw her curled up against the foot of her bed. Her hair was all tangled and she had her face in her hands. I rushed to her side, but had to peel her fingers away before she would look at me. 'Oh, no!' I scanned the apartment for a sign of Jairo, but he was nowhere to be seen. The place had seen some violence, too: chairs upturned and a saucepan lying beneath a missing chunk in the wall. My old beat box had hit the floor once again. This time it was beyond repair.

'He said I must've known you were splitting the money.' She spoke so faintly I had to watch her lips move. Much of her face was swollen and grazed, one eye closed up completely. Her top was ripped too, and I saw some angry scratch marks. 'Sonny, he did some things and blamed you for it. He said I deserved to be punished for giving birth to you. He took my money, took everything from me—' I held her tight as she began to howl and shudder, not giving a damn now that she had seen me with a gun.

'Everything is going to be OK,' I promised her, wishing she could be the one who said all this to me. 'I'll look after you from now on. You won't have to work any more. That's finished now, behind you. We'll move away from here. We can take off just like Papa. I'll earn enough to get us out of this city, over the mountains maybe.'

'What if he comes back?' My mother pulled away to look at me, but I had seen enough.

'Jairo is a dead man,' I assured her. 'You won't see him again.'

18

From the back of the cab next morning, I told Manu that I wouldn't need a jab this time. I saw his weird eyes shift into the rear-view mirror, and find me there.

'What's got into you?' he asked, frowning now. 'Suddenly you're in charge of the situation?'

'Something like that.' I turned my attention to the window, caught a glimpse of the Rio Medellín, shimmering behind two blocks. The river cut through the heart of the city, but Manu kept turning this way and that, and I soon lost sight of it. I didn't know where we were heading, but that was nothing new. I was just grateful that Manu had shown up at all. After the raid on the compound, part of me wondered whether I would ever see him again. That morning I had hung around the *barrio*, hoping to catch sight of him. I also kept an eye out for my uncle, dreaming of the moment when I put a hole the size of a coin between his eyes. He had left my mother with nothing, knocked all her dreams out of her. Despite years of practice using me as his punch bag, it seemed Jairo didn't care that his violence would be there for all to see. Part of me believed this was because he knew we would catch up with each other eventually. It was like *El Fantasma* said: you had to let go of all hope if you wanted to get on in this life. I may have only started to believe this for myself when I ran into Beatriz and her new man the evening before, but it was gospel to me now.

Sometimes Manu would chatter like only a cab driver could, and today was no exception. He had tuned in to hear the news, said yesterday's raid would throw up some stories very soon.

'No matter what side of the law you're on, you don't cross with the boss. It's just the way things are.'

I mumbled in agreement, but wasn't really listening. I had left Mamá resting in bed with some fruit juice fresh from the market, and told her that I couldn't stay at home today. She had wept some more and touched my face, but said she understood. I had stayed up late, the night before, sitting at her bedside just watching her sleep. I was sure that Jairo wouldn't be back. What worried me was the thought that every rise and fall of her chest under the blanket might be her last. It made me feel more tired than ever before as Manu drove me to work. I knew a jab would focus me but just couldn't take any more. I was sick of how lifeless it left me feeling, and figured I was old enough now to handle the hit straight. I could pull the trigger with my eyes closed, if I wanted, and hoped perhaps he knew that already. As Manu continued to comment on the news, I was content just to plug into my personal stereo and let Kurt sing me to sleep. It was good to be back in the taxi, feeling safe and sound for a while.

I woke up with a jolt. The CD had finished, but I still tugged out my phones like it had been feeding me nightmares. Manu had just switched off the engine, though he was still listening to the radio: one of those old country *vallenato* songs that only sounded good at weddings and wakes. I turned to my window, half listening to Manu hum along with the accordion, and gasped at what I saw.

I had never seen Medellín like this before, and realised we were up in the mountains. It looked like some kind of urban landslide down there: a city that had slipped off the slopes and into the vast valley below. A little mist wreathed the tangle of buildings and the boulevards, while the scrapers in the business centre looked like shards of sky. The whole place was so much bigger than I ever imagined, and so dense, but what really knocked me back was that it looked completely natural: just a part of the world we were in. The rooftops may have been the colour of rust, but there were palms crammed into all the streets and squares, with vines and creepers everywhere. I wound down the window, heard crickets in the long grass. We were parked up on a dirt track, just before a hairpin bend. I had missed quite a journey, I realised, nothing too steep but long and winding. I asked Manu what we were doing here. He just shrugged and shook his head.

'We're on time,' he told me. 'That's all I know.'

'Can I get out?'

'Sure.'

Manu joined me on the verge, and for a moment we stood there without speaking. The breeze on my face felt warm but clean, as if it had sailed right over the city. I spotted the stadium and the hospital, all the places I had been. If I listened carefully, I could make out car horns, a dog bark, then a dumper truck at work in the rubbish fields down from here, but none of it could shatter the sense of calm and peace. This was better than church, and I sensed my driver was just as impressed.

'Everyone in Medellín should see what it looks like from here,' I said. 'I never realised it could be so beautiful.'

'Most people never get out,' he replied. 'You're one of the lucky ones.'

What he said made me think of the reason we had travelled out so far. Any passing traffic would have trouble steering round the taxi, even a mule or a motorbike, so I guessed we were here for some kind of ambush. When I heard the sound of an engine struggling, I was almost sorry to think I'd be on my way home soon.

'Are you sure about that jab?' asked Manu.

'I made up my mind already,' I told him. I looked down the track, adjusting my holster as I turned, and saw a silver jeep crawl into view.

'Could I have a smoke instead?' I asked, as he prepared to light one himself. Manu looked at me from the corner of his good eye, the cigarette tip still cupped.

'Sure,' he said. 'Why not? Take this one.'

He sparked it up for me. I took a long, deep drag, thinking beyond what was expected of me now. It was just the hit I needed.

I had expected the 4x4 to pull up to the bumper, but it stopped some way down. I watched the driver's door spring open, and a figure jumped down who looked familiar to me. It wasn't until he opened the door behind him that I realised it was one of the guards from the compound. By then, two unmistakable white sneakers had dropped to the ground. I glanced at Manu, but he kept his eyes fixed on the boss.

'Shorty, I got something for you.' *El Fantasma* stopped to greet me half way. I noticed that he wasn't smoking a joint for once, but his manner seemed as easy as ever. He reached inside his jacket, and handed me an envelope.

'It's the season ticket I promised. Don't open it now. Let's take care of business first.'

'Thank you,' I said, trying to hide my surprise, and folded the envelope into the back of my jeans. I still had our tickets for the first match of the season in there: a prize that meant nothing to me now.

'You earned it,' he said, clapping me on the shoulder. 'And I *never* break my promise.' He stopped there for a moment and took in the view as I had. A blanket of pine trees fringed the rubbish fields, but I could work out where they began by all the turkey vultures. There they were, turning circles in the air with spread wings barely moving. I never thought birds like that could look so graceful, but then I had never seen them from above. I thought about Alberto, as I always did nowadays. Maybe he hadn't made it over the mountains, just like he dreamed, but the ridge was still a long way up and I believed he would've settled for this. It was impossible not to admire Medellín from here, and I could tell it touched *El Fantasma* too by the way he filled his lungs with air. I was just about to ask him what he wanted me for today when he came back around, said: 'I heard about your mother.'

'You did?'

'I want you to know I'll take care of her from now on. How is she?'

I told him she'd pull through, amazed that one man could know so much in a city so big and be so generous.

'I'd love for her to see this,' I said, and faced the city again.

Glancing back at the boss, I had thought he would be enjoying it, too. Instead, I found his eyes were on me still.

'I apologise for the rush to leave yesterday. My friends

at the precinct have let me down a little lately, but I can overcome that. I just have to restructure, make some transfers so we're playing to the best of our abilities.' As he spoke, I noticed the guard walk around to the other side of the jeep. 'Doesn't matter how badly I want to keep a player, Shorty, it all comes down to money.' *El Fantasma* moved aside now, turning just as a second figure emerged from the back of the vehicle. It was the last person I had expected to see, but I wasn't sorry he was here. I took a final drag on my cigarette and crushed it underfoot. 'Given the circumstances,' the boss continued, 'I couldn't refuse the first offer that came to me.'

Uncle Jairo took some time to join us. The slope wasn't steep, but it left him short of breath.

'What am I paying for here?' he wheezed, avoiding my eyes as he drew level with *El Fantasma*. 'I was expecting more than a friendly chat.'

'You'll get your money's worth.' The boss seemed offended by his manner. 'I was just explaining to your nephew how everyone has their price.'

'Lucky I came into some cash, really.' Jairo must have known I was wise to the fact that he was paying for this from Mamá's stolen purse. First he wiped a drop of spittle from the corner of his mouth, and suddenly he was grinning at me like this was a reunion. 'Take Galán, your store keeper buddy. I tell him I got a score I need to settle, some dude not being straight with me. It costs me enough to hurt, but sure enough he directs me straight to your man.'

My boss offered me this look, like my uncle had given

him a headache all the way here, but he wasn't alone in wanting to head off now. I was ready, had been so since my best friend disappeared, but this was the wake-up I needed.

I sensed cold sweat needle the back of my neck, a first for me as I reached for my gun, but it seemed right. Free now from that tranquillising jab, I felt more alive than ever before. I found my holster and the pop-down strap, then the pistol grip. At the same time, I saw the guard beckon yet another passenger from the car, someone so small I doubted he had been able to see over the dashboard.

'I have myself a new signing.' *El Fantasma* jabbed a thumb over his shoulder, watching my shooting hand still. He spoke breezily, like he was simply making conversation. 'He's a little green, but it's like I always say, there's nothing more unsettling than a kid with a gun.'

It wasn't the presence of another boy that surprised me, nor the fact that he was so much younger: seven, maybe eight years old. It was the weapon he clutched across his chest: a sub-machine gun of some sort. The piece was so big he looked almost ridiculous. It also meant the boss was right once again.

The guard bent down and spoke to him. The child nodded a few times, and then turned two tight blue eyes on me. We were some distance apart, but I could see that he was wired. Once again, I was glad I hadn't taken the jab. It meant I was free to think clearly, and not just about this moment. Mostly I thought about Nacional, but I didn't dwell on how they'd fare this season. That I had supported them with all my heart was all that mattered now. I felt the same about my mother, Alberto before me and Beatriz, too. Hope just didn't come into it for me any more. Only love.

'Be a man about this, Sonny. It's a noble way to go.' *El Fantasma* moved away from my uncle, creating a space for the boy behind him. 'Please don't think I overlooked your wings,' he added. 'I heard what you did for Alberto's family. In my book, you've earned them already.'

I sensed Manu retreat as he spoke, heard the taxi door open and close, the radio volume rise inside. Uncle Jairo didn't look like he agreed with *El Fantasma* one bit, but he always did know when to keep his mouth shut. Still facing my boss and my father's brother, I levelled my gun with both hands and clicked the hammer into place.

'It's time,' I agreed, nodding now because this felt like the only way to go. I wasn't sure how many bullets remained in the chamber, just so long as there was one. Killing Jairo would be too easy, I decided. I wanted him to see what I could do, because I knew that it would haunt him into the next life and beyond. The kid was looking very twitchy indeed, but he was only following my lead. Whether or not he was ready, this would make a man of him – just as it had done for Alberto and then me. I found the trigger, also a point above them all where the mountains met the sky. 'OK,' I breathed, and touched the muzzle to my temple. 'Let's finish this.'

Acknowledgements

Shortly before I sat down to write this book, I lost two people central to my life. Within the space of a few weeks, my mother and younger sister passed away. It was a dark time. Death became a part of me. It influenced every thought and feeling, and that included the kind of story I wanted to tell.

In *Boy Kills Man*, I had no idea whether such a short rage against unfairness and injustice would ever see the light of day. My previous novels were light-hearted comedies, and yet this was something I had to write. It's not about grief but inevitability. Quite simply, I wanted to explore how it felt to be in possession of a gun at a formative time of life. In a heartbeat, that weapon would come to heighten your awareness of the world around you and ultimately shape your destiny. In my mind, that seemed no different to living with a terminal illness. No matter what, it gets you in the end.

Ten years on, I still don't think of this as a bleak book. The narrator is a minor. He's at an age where death is not on his radar. Life is everything, even in a region of the world at a time when all the odds are stacked against him. So when the means to make things happen presents itself, he seizes the opportunity.

After six weeks of intense writing, I remember finishing the last sentence as if it were yesterday. Straight away, I had an urge to leave my desk to get some air. It was a warm, clear afternoon. I sat on a bench and stayed there for an hour. It felt good to be outside.

Over the course of a decade, many people have humbled me with their passion for this book. I should like to thank Philippa Milnes-Smith and David Godwin, Emily Thomas and Venetia Gosling, Honor Wilson-Fletcher, Kirsty Mclachlan, Mary Byrne, Elena Sanchez (for the colour), Melvin Burgess, Emma Whyman, Sarah Odedina and all at Hot Key Books for this anniversary edition.

About the Author

Matt Whyman is the author of several critically acclaimed novels, including *The Savages* and *American Savage*, as well as two comic memoirs, *Pig in the Middle* and *Walking with Sausage Dogs*. He is married and lives with his family in West Sussex.

HOT KEY BOOKS

Thank you for choosing a Hot Key book.

If you want to know more about our authors and what we publish, you can find us online.

You can start at our website

www.hotkeybooks.com

And you can also find us on:

We hope to see you soon!